KARMA

Karma

A Mystery in Paris

MARILYN FREEMAN

*With Best Wishes
To Olive

Marilyn Freeman*

Spellbrooktales

- (c) 2021 Copyright Marilyn Freeman

- All rights reserved, no part of this book may be published, stored in a retrieval system, transmitted, in any form of binding or cover than that in which it is published, without the written permission of the author, Marilyn Freeman, except in the case of brief reviews or other permitted uses under copyright law.

- **NOTE**: All characters and events in this publication, other than those clearly in the public domain are fictitious and any resemblance to real persons, living or dead, is purely coincidental.

- *Published by Spellbrooktales*

- ISBN: 978-1-8384260-0-2

Contents

Text Insert iv

1. Karma — 1
2. The Funeral — 5
3. The Postcard — 10
4. The Dinner — 16
5. Journey to Paris — 23
6. Janey, Paris 11th March 1962 — 27
7. Francois, Paris 1952 — 35
8. Francois and Clemence, 1953 — 46
9. Armand, Paris 1953 — 51

10	Janey, Paris, March 1962.	60
11	The Meeting, Paris, March 12th 1962	70
12	Wembley 11th March 1962	77
13	Paris, 1972	84
14	Francois and Adrienne Meet in Paris	90
15	Prefecture de Police	100
16	The Private Detective	106
17	The Wait for News	113
18	A Body in the Seine	120
19	The Police Search	126
20	Two Days in Paris	133
21	News From the Archives	137
22	Lauren	147
23	Lauren's Story	153

24	The Plan	158
25	The Finale	163
26	Karma	170
About The Author		176

Chapter 1

Karma

March 1972

The sky was deep blue, and the white cliffs sparkled in the sunlight and Adrienne Grainger was lost in thought as she leant against the rail on the rear deck of the cross-channel ferry heading to France. She could have gone down to the restaurant for lunch, but instead, felt she needed time to reflect on all that had happened to her in the past few short weeks. Weeks when her life had changed forever....

It was Friday at last and she had been looking forward to the weekend. For some reason, it had been a particularly demanding week at school. At that moment, in the distance, she saw her great aunt Marge, step out of their front door and walk quickly to the gate. She stood at the edge of the pavement and glanced up the road to check it was clear. Then, noticing Adrienne, gave her a wave and indicated that she was going to the corner shop. Marge failed to look the other way again and tragically, never saw the car as it sped around the corner. As she stepped into the road the driver jumped on the brakes. They squealed and Marge turned her head, only to see, far too late, that she was directly in its path. The car slammed into her with a sickening thud.

Adrienne watched in horror as, in slow motion it seemed, Marge was lifted high in the air, somersaulting onto the car roof before sliding off as the driver hit the accelerator and drove away, leaving Marge with her head on the kerb and her body akimbo in the road.

For a second there was silence, then she heard herself screaming 'Noooo! No!' as she ran along the road towards Marge's stricken body. She dropped down beside her, but to her horror, could see that the colour was already draining from her aunt's face.

A few people had emerged from their houses and someone said they had phoned for the ambulance. After endless minutes, she heard the siren. Adrienne knew it was hopeless, but they had to try to save her. They carefully placed her on a stretcher and lifted her into the ambulance. Adrienne went with her to the hospital. She was taken straight to a bay in the Accident and Emergency department. They tried to massage her heart and gave her mouth-to-mouth resuscitation, but it was no good. The blood trickling from her ears told the story. She had suffered a massive brain injury and must, they said, have died the instant she hit the floor.

Everyone at the hospital had been very kind. So had the policeman who questioned her. Did she see the car? Did she see the driver? Had she noticed the number? She only knew it was a black car with shaded windows and no, she hadn't noticed the number she told him. It all happened so fast. The only thing she could remember, was that slow-motion image of Marge flying through the air that was playing around and around in her brain.

Adrienne got out of the taxi that someone at the hospital had kindly called for her. As she walked up the short path to the front door, she noticed it was still slightly ajar, as Marge must have left it, and for one brief moment she expected to find her in the kitchen making supper. As she pushed open the kitchen door, grief gripped her like an awful cramp in the pit of her stomach. Nausea swept over her; she rushed for the sink and was violently sick.

They had asked her whether there was anyone they could call, to be with her, but as she told them, there was no-one. There was only Aunt Marge and she was gone. Exhausted, she eventually collapsed into bed and tried to sleep, without success. What would she do without her? Marge had cared for Adrienne since that dreadful day when her mother hadn't come home. No-one ever knew why, or where she had gone. Of course, they did look for her. Photos were posted in shops, outside the police station, at the railway station; anywhere, in fact, where people passed by, in the hope that someone, somewhere, may have seen her. No-one had, and Adrienne became an orphan at the age of twelve without ever knowing how or why.

For years she had looked for her on every street, searched for her from bus windows, waited in vain at the gate just in case she should come walking round the corner. Gradually, she came to accept that her mother was gone, and that was that. Even now after all these years though, there was still a part of her that longed for her. Now she was truly alone.

The police searched for the driver, of course, but they didn't have much to go on. So far, the only witness was herself and she remembered little. The days before the funeral were black. She barely functioned. She made the arrangements with the undertaker without really knowing what she was doing. She placed the announcement in the classified Births, Deaths and Marriages, but didn't know why. Tradition, she supposed. After all, there wasn't really anyone to inform. Adrienne had never found it easy to make friends. To make a close friend meant opening up feelings that had long since been buried. Best to keep a tight grip on emotions, so that's what she had done for years. Only Aunt Marge, who had shared the loss of her mother, had been allowed in behind the protective wall she had built around herself. Now Marge was gone.

Chapter 2

The Funeral

The day of the funeral dawned incongruously bright. Adrienne had slept only fitfully, each wakeful hour filled with thoughts of the day ahead. Would she hold it together while she read out the short tribute? Not that there would be many people to hear it. Marge hadn't had many friends either and even fewer relations. A few people who had worked with her over the years, and a distant cousin or two, had let her know they were coming, but that was it. Adrienne knew none of them personally.

At eight, she finally gave up on further sleep, slid out of bed and padded into the bathroom. After a long hot shower she felt a little more able to face the day and went downstairs to make herself a strong black coffee. She couldn't face food right now. She felt so alone, sitting at the table in the kitchen. This was where she and Marge had begun their days for as long as she could remember. They would chat idly over breakfast about the coming day, and she knew she would desperately miss all that; sharing her life with someone else.

Marge was to be buried in the family plot in the Alperton Cemetery, with her sister, Adrienne's grandmother. The thought crossed her mind that her mother should probably be there too. She had almost given up hope that she might still be alive somewhere. If she had been, Adrienne was sure she would have come back to her.

She went back upstairs and mechanically dried her hair and applied her make-up. She glanced at the new black dress hanging behind the door. Normally, she would never wear black, which did nothing for her pale complexion and mousey hair, and she'd had to buy one for the occasion. She pulled it over her head without enthusiasm and looked disapprovingly at herself in the mirror.

The service in the chapel in the middle of the cemetery was brief. A couple of hymns, weakly sung to the piped music, by the eight or so people present; a short address, full of largely irrelevant words, by the vicar who had been hired in for the occasion, and her tribute, and that was it. As she followed the coffin out of the church, she smiled wanly at the few people who were there. They were all in some way connected to Marge, but all strangers to her. Not much of a send-off, she thought, for someone who had meant so much to her. But she had done her best.

Now, as she stood by the graveside feeling utterly bereft, she noticed a stranger standing a little way off.

It was a man. He looked to be in his fifties. He hadn't been in the church and she was sure she'd never seen him before. Maybe he was someone who had worked with Marge. He remained at a distance as she accepted the condolences offered by the other mourners. Dismissing him from her mind she thanked the vicar and turned to walk back to her car.

'Adrienne?' A man's voice penetrated her consciousness. She turned and saw that the man by the graveside had followed her.

'Adrienne, I'm so sorry for your loss,' he said quietly. His voice had a slightly 'continental' accent. It could have been French, she thought.

'Thank you,' replied Adrienne politely, but wondered who on earth this person was. What was a perfect stranger doing here, and now, of all times?

'I'm sorry, do I know you?' she went on.

'No, unfortunately you don't,' he replied, and Adrienne couldn't help noticing the sadness in his voice, and something else; was it regret?

'Who are you? Were you a friend of Marge's?' she asked nervously, beginning to resent the intrusion of this stranger at this time of such personal grief.

'No, I didn't actually know her, but can't you guess who I am?' he said, seemingly reluctant to say out loud what must be said.

'Please!' Adrienne retorted, 'How do you know me?'

'I'm your father,' he said, so softly that Adrienne could hardly hear the words.

Adrienne reeled, her legs buckled, and she would

have slid to the ground had he not caught her arm in support. Her father! She'd never felt that she even had a father! Her mother had hardly ever spoken of 'a father' and then only to dismiss the possibility that she would ever meet him.

Shrugging his hand away, she managed

'But how, why?'

'I'm sorry to spring this on you,' the man said quickly, 'I saw the announcement in the paper, and I wanted to see you, to explain, and I hoped ...'

'Hoped what!' Adrienne exclaimed, surprised by her own angry reaction. 'You have a nerve, to turn up here after all these years. Twenty-two years and I barely even knew you existed! After Mum disappeared there was just me and Aunty Marge. Where were you then? You must have seen the newspaper articles and posters about Mum. Why didn't you contact us then?'

'I've been overseas for the past ten years. I've only just come back from the Far East, so I didn't know anything about your Mum's disappearance. I'm so sorry Adrienne.'

Adrienne couldn't make any sense of this. She was an orphan. She'd been an orphan for ten years. Her mind could not absorb the information he was giving her. Could this stranger really be her father? She felt so angry she wanted to scream at him, but at the same time she felt something else. What was this feeling? Was it hope? Fear?

'I just want to get to know you, if you'll let me Adrienne,' he whispered softly.

'Look, I can't think straight right now,' Adrienne retorted, 'You'll have to give me time to take all this in. How do I know you are my father anyway?'

He reached into the inside pocket of his jacket and pulled out a photograph, faded and a little frayed at the edges, but it was of her mother holding her in her arms and standing beside a man whose face could have been a younger version of the face of the man standing before her now.

Still she couldn't take it in. If this really was her father, what did he want from her?

'Look, I can't deal with this now. Give me your number and perhaps I'll call you in a week or two,' she said sharply.

'Of course, I understand,' the man said. He tore a page out of a small notebook and wrote down the name and telephone number of his hotel. 'I'll be staying here for the next few weeks, in Room 10. Goodbye for now, Adrienne,' he said gently, and then turned quickly on his heels and walked away.

Adrienne stood for some moments. Part of her wanted to run after him. She had so many questions, but they would have to wait. She realised she needed to give herself time to grieve for Marge before getting involved with this virtual stranger. Too late, she realised that she didn't even know his name.

Chapter 3

The Postcard

Several days passed. The haze of grief began to clear a little and Adrienne thought once more about the stranger at the graveside. Still, though, she wasn't ready to face him. It just seemed too huge right then. She decided to give it a few more weeks before ringing him.

After a couple of weeks, Adrienne turned her attention to dealing with Marge's financial affairs and sorting out her effects. Money wasn't an issue. It turned out that Marge had left her the house, her not insubstantial savings, her jewellery and, well, just about everything else.

She needed to check through Marge's papers for information for the insurance company and decided to look in the large black box file on top of the wardrobe. It was heavy, and she struggled to lift it down. She was balancing precariously on a footstool to reach it and as she took hold of it, she wobbled, and it slipped from her fingers, spreading its contents unceremoniously across the floor.

'Damn!' said Adrienne impatiently. She jumped down and began to gather up what seemed like hundreds of bits of paper. She was picking them up one by one, trying to match up any pieces that seemed to be related and was about halfway through when she came across a postcard. On the front were pictures she recognised as the Eiffel Tower, the Arc de Triomphe, Notre Dame and the Sacre Coeur, arranged around the word 'Paris'. She turned it over and her stomach churned.

The writing looked familiar, but it was the name at the bottom that sprang out. Janey, her mother's name! Marge had always referred to her as Janey. At the top Janey had written the date 11th March 1962, the day her mother had walked out of the house, never to return. She sank to the floor, hardly able to breathe. Her mother had gone to Paris! Not only that, but at some point, Marge had known that she had, and said nothing!

Her mind was now doing cartwheels. Why hadn't Marge told her about this postcard? Why had her mother left without a word? What had happened to her to stop her from coming home? She eagerly read the message on the card, hoping it might answer at least some of her questions.

It read;

'Marge,

I'm sorry I had to lie to you in my note. In fact, I wanted to let you know I'm actually here in Paris, staying at L'Hotel Grande, Rue Mazarine, but I'm alright. I hope you and Adrienne are OK. I'm sorry I had to leave without telling you everything, but I know it was for the best and I'll explain it all when I get back. I'm meeting someone soon who will give me the answers I need and hopefully, I'll be home next week.

Love Janey.

Sitting there on the bedroom floor, she had gone through the whole gamut of emotions. She was moved to tears to see her mother's name in her own hand. They ran silently down her cheeks as she felt herself reach out to her mother across the years. How often had she longed for some contact with her? And now, although this was only a tentative connection, it was after all, a newly discovered link to her mother. It brought half-forgotten memories, of the feel of her arms around her, the smell of her hair and the sound of her voice whispering goodnight.

Dragging herself back into the present, feelings of anger rose in her chest. She was furious that this postcard had been here for all those years, while she had been yearning for news of her mother. How could Marge have kept it from her? Why did she go on pretending that she had no idea where Janey was? Was she trying to let her forget her mother? If so, she hadn't succeeded. Well, Marge wasn't around to ask so maybe she would have to assume she had her reasons.

She got slowly to her feet and began to tidy up the papers. She felt at a loss as to what to do with this mind-numbing information. Should she, could she, simply put the postcard back in the box and try to forget about it? She instantly dismissed that thought. She would never be able to forget it. She already knew that she had to find out what happened to prevent Janey from coming home all those years ago. Was there more information somewhere in this pile of papers?

She picked up and inspected each document before placing it neatly back in the box. After half an hour she picked up the final piece but had found nothing. There were no more postcards or letters from her mother, no photographs that might give her more clues, nothing.

Where on earth could she go from here, she wondered. With a start she realised that perhaps there was someone who may be able to help her. Could the stranger at the graveside, who had said he was her father, know something? Could he hold any clues? Searching through her handbag she found the piece of paper where he had written the name and phone number of his hotel. Checking her watch, she saw it was ten o'clock. Far too late to ring him now. She determined to leave it until the morning.

At six-thirty, after a disturbed night's sleep, she dragged herself out of bed. She went through the motions of washing and dressing without really thinking what she was doing. Her mind was full of questions about that postcard and how soon she would be able to ring the man who claimed to be her father. She realised once more that she didn't even know his name.

She paced around, tried to read her book, wrote a

shopping list, made another cup of tea – anything to occupy herself until it was a reasonable time for her to ring him. What if he'd already left! She was kicking herself that she hadn't tried to contact him sooner. At ten o'clock she could wait no longer. With a trembling hand she dialled the number he had given her.

'The Metropole Hotel, how can I help you?' the lady's voice at the other end of the line asked.

As she didn't have his name, she asked for the gentleman in room 10.

'Ah yes, Mr De Havilland. I'm putting you through now.'

'Hello?' a rather smooth yet strong voice answered.

'Oh hello,' Adrienne answered, astonished that her voice had almost disappeared. Clearing her throat, she began 'It's Adrienne here,' and then, all in a rush, 'I wonder, could we meet?'

'Adrienne! How lovely to hear from you. Yes, of course, I would love to see you.'

'Shall I come to the hotel?' Adrienne asked tentatively.

'Yes, of course. Can you come for dinner, say about seven?' he replied enthusiastically.

Adrienne hesitated briefly, unsure whether 'dinner' would be too intimate a situation but decided that at least it would give them time to talk.

'Err, OK, I'll see you at seven.' she managed, then put the phone down, rather too quickly, she felt afterwards. Well, she'd done it. She'd spoken to her 'father'. Mr De Havilland! At least she had a surname, but still she didn't know his first name. She wondered how she would address him. She couldn't call him father or Dad and Mr De Havilland sounded too formal. She decided she would just have to play it by ear.

She couldn't help feeling nervous, or was it excitement? Was he really her father? What would he be like? Would he know anything about her mother? She knew that the odds were, that by the time Janey disappeared, they hadn't met for many years, and that he quite possibly knew nothing about why she was in Paris in 1962. Still, however remote the possibility, she knew she had to find out because at that moment she herself had no clue.

Chapter 4

The Dinner

She rang her hairdresser for an appointment. She felt she had to make an effort. This could be one of the most important meetings of her life and she wanted to look her best. She chose a smart yet modest blue dress which matched her eyes and was her favourite. As she stepped out to get into the taxi, she knew she looked good and that gave her confidence.

'Hotel Metropole in the High Street, please,' she said to the taxi driver.

'Ok miss,' he replied.

The journey took about ten minutes. She paid the taxi driver and stepped onto the pavement. She stood for a moment or two, composing herself, before striding purposefully toward the hotel entrance.

It was rather a splendid foyer, all large mirrors and shining brass lamp fittings above a plush burgundy carpet. Luxurious sofas were dotted around expensive brass and glass coffee tables. He was obviously waiting for her to arrive and stood up as she came through the double doors. He strode towards her with outstretched hand.

'Adrienne,' he said, smiling, 'I'm so glad you're here.'

She shook his hand and said 'Hello,' and then 'I'm sorry, I don't know your name.'

'I'm so sorry, I should have introduced myself when we last met. I'm Francois De Havilland.'

'Francois, that's a French name isn't it?' she asked quickly.

'It is. I was born in Paris, but I've travelled all over the place. I think of myself as a citizen of the world if that doesn't sound too grand!'

The Paris connection wasn't lost on Adrienne and her hopes rose that perhaps he may be able to help her after all. He ordered a bottle of French Claret, without even asking her what she would like to drink, which annoyed her slightly. He seems very sure of himself, she thought. Still, she had to admit, it was rather a good wine and she began to relax a little.

'I thought we could eat here, and I've booked us a table for seven-thirty,' he said, 'if that's ok for you?'

'Yes,' she replied, 'it looks very nice.'

She thought that it also looked very expensive. They sipped their wine in a rather awkward silence. Finally Adrienne asked

'Do you still live in Paris?'

'Not really,' he said. 'To be honest, I haven't decided where I'll settle down yet. My job in Singapore has finished and now I have to find myself something else, and somewhere to live. I'm not in any hurry though,'

'I see,' she said.

She was growing impatient to start the conversation about her mother. That was why she was here after all, not just to exchange pleasantries with this perfect stranger, and yet something was holding her back. She was so desperate to find out if he knew anything that she was almost afraid to bring the subject up in case the answer was 'no'.

An official looking chap in a tuxedo appeared and announced that their table was ready.

'Thank you,' Francois replied and gestured to Adrienne to follow the Maitre D into the dining room.

They had been given a table in a quiet corner and as Adrienne approached, the Maitre D pulled out a chair and gestured to her to sit down. Unused to such formal behaviour she felt a little awkward but sat down as he slid the chair beneath her.

Francois had collected their wine glasses from the foyer and now placed her drink in front of her.

They both chose Steak Diane. She felt very sophisticated in these opulent surroundings but a little out of her depth if she was honest. They chatted throughout the meal about this and that. He was interested in her job at the local primary school and she was happy enough to talk about the antics of her young charges. Still, all the while, she was aching to ask him the one question to which she needed an answer, and that was, when did he last see or hear from her mother?

Finally, the meal was over, and he asked her was there some particular reason why she had rung and asked to meet him. Relieved that he had opened up the subject, she blurted out the whole story about finding the postcard from Paris and the message it bore. Francois looked puzzled at first, and then rather taken aback.

'I wanted to ask you; did you know anything about Mum going to Paris in '62?' she asked. 'I need to find out what happened to her to stop her from coming home.'

He seemed genuinely shocked and said 'Paris '62 did you say?'

'Yes, does that mean anything to you?'

'What date was that?'

'The 11th March 1962,' Adrienne replied, a little breathlessly.

'Well, on the 12th March I received a postcard from your mother out of the blue asking to meet me at a certain café just off the Rue de St Germain-des-Pres that evening, at eight. It said nothing about why she wanted to see me. I kind of assumed it might be something about you. Well, I went along to the café at about 7.30pm but she never turned up.'

'Did she let you know why?' Adrienne demanded.

'That was the strange thing,' he said, 'I never heard anything else from her. I had no address or telephone number for her and just waited for her to get in touch again, but I heard nothing. A week later I was due to fly out to Singapore to start my new job, so I had to assume she'd changed her mind about seeing me.'

Adrienne was shocked, frustrated, and angry with him because he hadn't tried to find Janey.

'Surely there must have been something you could have done. Why didn't you go to the police?' she almost shouted. People had begun to stare at them.

Francois replied quietly,

'Obviously, I had no idea she might have come to harm. Remember, I hadn't seen or heard from her in years and had literally no contact details. I just had to let it go. I had no idea what she had wanted to talk about, no clue at all as to why she was even in Paris. I really couldn't think what I could do or even whether I needed to be doing anything!'

Adrienne felt utterly devastated. She had thought that she might have a chance of finding out what had happened to Janey, but now her hopes had been dashed once again. She desperately needed to be alone. She needed to think about what Francois had told her and there were now new questions buzzing around her head. How did her mother know that Francois was in Paris? He must have been the man she had referred to in the postcard, but he insisted that he didn't know why she wanted to see him. Had she known all along where Francois, her father, was and if so, why hadn't she told her about him? What was the reason that she'd had to leave her and Marge without even telling them that she was going to see Francois?

She thanked him for dinner and got up to leave.

'Look, I'm really sorry I can't tell you any more Adrienne. I know it must be a disappointment to you. Perhaps you'll never know what happened to her.'

'What! I can assure you, I'll never give up!' she said fiercely.

Francois looked a little taken aback by the ferocity of her response.

'Of course not,' he said quickly 'I didn't mean ....'

'Well, as long as there's breath in me, now that I know she was in Paris, I won't stop until I get some answers. Anyway, I really must go now.'

'Well, thanks once more for coming. Could we meet again? I'll be here for a few more weeks.'

Adrienne wasn't sure what to do but felt that she still needed to keep this connection going. There may be something else regarding her mother that may come to light she thought; and with that thought came another. What if Francois wasn't being entirely honest with her. It seemed an incredible coincidence that he had turned up at this moment in time, just as she had discovered the French connection. However, after a moment or two she said,

'Ok, perhaps I'll give you a ring in a day or two.'

'Good,' he said. 'I'll organise a taxi for you.'

With that, he ushered her towards reception and asked the girl behind the desk to call the taxi company.

Five minutes later, he escorted her to the taxi waiting outside the front door, shook her hand rather formally and said,

'Goodnight Adrienne, I'll be waiting for your call.'

She quickly removed her hand from his and mumbled,

'Yes, thanks again,' before hurriedly stepping inside the taxi.

'21 Penvale Avenue' she called out to the driver, and then immediately felt uneasy that Francois might have heard her address. Now, why does that bother me? she thought.

Chapter 5

Journey to Paris

As Adrienne lay in bed that night her head was full of questions. There were so many things that were not adding up. Paris, why Paris? Why the secrecy? Did Francois know more than he was telling her. He seemed genuine enough, and yet, there was something.

She made a decision. She knew it was a long shot, but she would go to Paris and try to find out what had happened to Janey. But where to begin? She realised there were a couple of places she could start, and they were the hotel where she had stayed and possibly the last place where anyone had seen her, the cafe where she was meant to meet Francois. She also realised she would need him to tell her where that was, which meant seeing him again. She decided to ring him first thing in the morning. The following weekend would be the start of the Easter holiday break. She would have at least three weeks to spend in Paris. Surely, she should be able to get somewhere in that time.

The next morning she rang the hotel and asked to

speak to Mr De Havilland. As she was waiting to be put through, she belatedly wondered whether he would think she was being rather too keen, but it was too late to worry about that now. He said 'Hello' a bit hesitantly as though he wasn't expecting a phone call.

'It's Adrienne' she replied, a little nervously, 'I'm sorry to bother you this early but I have something I have to ask you.'

'Ask away,' he said, 'And thank you for coming last evening, it was lovely getting to know you a little.'

'Oh, yes of course, thanks for dinner by the way.'

'My pleasure. So what can I do for you?'

'Look, I've decided that I must go to Paris to try to find out what happened to Mum and one of the few clues I have right now is the place she arranged to meet you. Can you tell me where that was?'

There were a few seconds of silence before Francois answered her.

'Are you sure Adrienne? It's a long time ago. Whatever trail there was will have gone cold by now, surely.'

Adrienne felt a wave of anger rise in her chest.

'Am I sure? How can you ask me that? Ten long years I've waited to find out what happened to my mother; and now at last I have a clue, and nothing is going to stop me from following it up. Now, where were you meant to meet her?'

Again, a long silence followed and then,

'It was a cafe just off the Rue de St Germain-des-Pres. I can't actually remember the name, but I would know it if I saw it again. Look, if you are determined to go, I'll try to help you.'

'Are you intending to go back to Paris then?'

'Well, I could be. I do have some other business to attend to, so I was planning to fly over there next week anyway. When were you thinking of going?'

Adrienne hadn't made a final decision about how and when to travel to Paris and pulled back a little, saying,

'Well, I hadn't actually got that far. I do have some holidays coming up ...'

'Well, look,' he interrupted, 'why don't I tell you where I'll be staying and when, and you can look me up when you get to Paris, if and when you need to?'

Somewhat reassured by this apparent retreat on his part, Adrienne readily agreed to this arrangement and gave him her phone number.

'When do you think you'll be leaving?' she enquired tentatively.

'I'll be flying out on Thursday morning. I'll ring you before I leave to give you the details of where to find me. I should be there for a couple of weeks at least.'

'OK, and thank you,' she said, feeling some gratitude that he at least had seemed to be willing to help her in her quest. And then, came the inevitable tiny element of doubt that always seemed to creep in after every conversation she had with him. Was it just coincidence that he had been intending to go to Paris in the next few days? Why hadn't he mentioned it during dinner last evening?

She shrugged off the feeling and ended the conversation in as cordial a manner as she could manage.

A week later she caught the early train to Dover. Settling in her seat, she checked that she had stowed her passport carefully and also the note on which she had written the information Francois had given her the previous week. He was staying at the Ritz, which had impressed her greatly. Whatever he had been doing in Singapore had obviously been pretty lucrative. She would contact him as soon as she got to Paris, as he held one of the few keys to her mother's last known whereabouts. Of course, she thought, a little uncomfortably, he knew that too.

Standing on the deck of the ferry, Adrienne felt that she was travelling between two worlds, the one full of sadness and unsolvable questions and the other where she would at last find answers and be able to move her life on. She felt she had been stuck in this limbo for long enough.

Finally, the French coast drew nearer, and it was time to prepare to disembark to catch the train to Paris. Once on board the train, she chose a window seat and settled down to enjoy the view of the French countryside.

Chapter 6

Janey, Paris 11th March 1962

Janey sat by the window on the Paris train, looking out onto the green fields of France. She noticed they were similar to the green fields of home except that there were fewer hedgerows and no hills. She was feeling anxious that she'd had to leave home without telling anyone, not even her beloved daughter Adrienne. Had she done the right thing? Even Marge was in the dark. Of course, she had left a note to say that she was going to see an old friend of hers in Wiltshire who had suddenly been taken ill. She hoped to be back before Marge started to make enquiries, and then she would be able to explain what was going on. In fact, she decided she would send a postcard when she got to Paris, so that they wouldn't be worrying about her.

She was feeling a mixture of emotions right now. She was excited at the prospect of possibly meeting the father she had long believed to be dead. She was nervous of the circumstances surrounding him. He was obviously living under some kind of threat, or why had the letter told her to 'tell no-one for her father's sake.'? Would she be walking into danger herself? She thought about Adrienne. Had she done the right thing in leaving her, to respond to the demand from a perfect stranger to embark upon this possibly dangerous journey? And yet, the pull had been too strong. The chance to find her father had been too difficult for her to resist.

The letter she'd received was explicit. No-one must know anything, for her father's sake. Her father's sake!? What could all this mean. As far as she knew her father had probably died in a German prisoner of war camp. At least that's what Aunt Marge had always told her. But he was still alive! The letter said that he was, but that he was in hiding somewhere in Paris. It didn't say why he was in hiding, only that he wanted to see her. It was all very mysterious; but most bewildering of all, it asked her to bring with her a bracelet which had turned up years before with no information as to who had sent it and no return address. It was a plain silver bracelet, but it had a series of numbers engraved on the inside. She had assumed they were something to do with a maker's mark or model number. When it arrived, she had decided it was from Adrienne's father, Francois, but as she had never heard from him since it had turned up, she really had no idea where it had come from.

Now, as she sat on the train on the way to Paris

thinking about all of this, she realised that as the years had passed, she had come to understand why Francois had cut all ties. Their relationship had been just another casualty of that terrible war. She knew that he couldn't have hurt his wife any more after all she had been through and Janey had always known that his first loyalty had been to her. Still, as the train hurtled towards Paris, a small part of her couldn't help wondering what it would be like to see him again. Coincidences do happen, she told herself. The possibility of bumping into him was of course remote, but the train of thought prompted the memory of the last time she had seen him. She had gone with him to St Pancras Station to say goodbye as he boarded the train to catch the ferry back to France. She had Adrienne with her who was just gone two years old. He'd kissed them both and promised to return in the next few weeks. She never saw him again.

They had met three years earlier when Francois was visiting friends in London. Janey was on her way to the Building Exhibition to research trends in post-war architecture for a thesis she was doing for her studies at the Architectural Association's School of Architecture. She and Francois literally bumped into each other outside the British Museum. The file she was carrying catapulted to the floor and he gallantly apologised and picked it up for her. He was a handsome young Frenchman and she was a pretty and intelligent young woman and the attraction was instantaneous.

The visit to the Building Exhibition was postponed for another day as was his day at the Museum. The next couple of weeks were spent in a romantic haze. They spent every hour together that they could. He told her that he had been married before the war but that his wife had disappeared in the turmoil of the German occupation of Paris. He hadn't heard from her since she left home to visit a friend in July 1942 and by now, he had to assume that she was no longer alive. This tragic story only added to the romance of the situation for Janey. They became lovers and when his visit was at an end, he swore that he would return as soon as he could.

After a few weeks, Janey realised that she was pregnant. She was horrified. This wasn't how her life was meant to progress. She was going to be an architect, and while she wanted children eventually, this was not the time for it to be happening. How could she tell Marge? Since her father had been left behind on the Dunkirk beaches in 1940 and her mother had died of a heart attack, her mother's Aunt Marge, even though she was unmarried herself, had taken her in and raised her as her own. She had struggled to make sure that she had a decent education and was so proud that Janey was 'going to make something of herself'. Her gaining a place at the AA was a source of great pride for Marge, and for herself too. Now that dream would come to a shuddering end. It would be impossible to continue her studies. She briefly considered trying to 'get rid of it' but dismissed the idea as soon as it formed. This was a life that was growing inside her and part of the man she loved, and she couldn't contemplate destroying it.

She immediately wrote to Francois and waited anxiously for his reaction. When it came, it wasn't what she had hoped for. He declared his love for her and said that if he had been free, he would of course, have married her. If he had been free!!! She was shaken to the core. She had believed that he was free as he hadn't seen his wife for nine years and seemed sure she was dead. However, he would have had to formally request that she be declared dead before he could remarry, and he couldn't bring himself to do that without having one last attempt at finding out what had happened to her.

Janey was devastated. His reassurance that he would help her out financially did little to assuage her anger. How could he do this to her? She was left with little alternative but to return home to Marge who was of course, utterly shocked. She had sacrificed a lot for Janey's education and now, in her eyes, she had thrown it all away on a holiday romance! Of course, as the baby grew inside Janey and became more of a reality her attitude softened. Together they prepared for the baby's appearance and by the time she went into labour they were ready to welcome it into the world. Janey gave birth to Adrienne, weighing in at a healthy eight pounds six ounces at 5.30am one cold January morning. She was perfect, with her own fair hair and blue eyes but also looking every inch her father's daughter.

Francois had been in touch a few times during her pregnancy but hadn't been able to visit. Four weeks after the birth he made the journey to see them and stayed for a couple of weeks getting to know his daughter. He promised to help to support his child and arranged for a sum to be paid into Janey's account each month. He visited a couple of times over the next year or so. Janey still hoped that once his wife was officially declared dead, he would marry her, and they would be a proper family.

Just after Adrienne's second birthday Francois came for a brief visit. He had a new lead that he was following up and seemed hopeful that he would be able to finally find out what had happened to his wife and then, he would be free. As he kissed Janey and Adrienne goodbye he promised to return as soon as he could.

Janey never saw him again. A letter arrived three weeks later with the news she had been dreading for so long. He had discovered what had become of his wife and she was still alive! Janey had felt sick when she read it. It was the end of all her happy-family dreams. Francois said that his wife had been taken off the street the day she had walked out of their apartment and shipped off to the east, placed in a labour camp and subjected to terrible mis-treatment. By the time the war ended she was so traumatised she hardly knew her own name, let alone where she had come from.

Released from the camp she had barely survived, getting work when she could, eating when she worked and virtually starving when she couldn't find any. He had finally found her in a Displaced Person's camp. He knew he must take care of her and brought her back to Paris. He also knew that after all she had been through, he could never tell her about Janey and Adrienne. He would not be returning to England. He wrote to Janey to explain all of this and she had been utterly devastated.

Janey had assumed that he would continue to help support his child, but a year later the payments stopped. She had tried to contact him to find out why, but her letters came back unopened. After three months trying to find Francois, she had given up and accepted that she would be bringing Adrienne up on her own. Of course, she was angry and disappointed that he had let her down after promising to help her but assumed that he must have decided to cut all ties with her and Adrienne because of his wife.

The bracelet had turned up just before the payments stopped. The parcel had a Paris postmark and in the absence of any other information as to who had sent it and with no return address, she had concluded it was from Francois, perhaps eventually meant for his daughter, maybe because he had decided to stop sending her money. She was so angry she couldn't bear to look at it and stuffed it to the back of a drawer.

Over the years, she had more or less forgotten all about it, until, that is, the letter, also with a Paris postmark, had turned up four days ago.

Now it appeared that the bracelet had not come from Francois at all. It must have come from her father, or someone close to him! Of course, this realisation prompted more questions than answers. If he had been alive then, why hadn't he tried to contact Janey's mother? Perhaps he had, as he may not have known she was dead. Now it turned out that he was still alive! Where had he been all these years, and why was he in hiding; from what or from whom?

The jolt of the train as it shuddered to a halt in the Gard Du Nord ended her reverie. As she gathered up her belongings, she told herself that hopefully, she would soon have her answers.

Chapter 7

Francois, Paris 1952

Francois stepped down onto Platform Six at the Gare du Nord and strode towards the metro station. He bought a ticket to Mabillon and boarded the Metro. Emerging into the daylight he walked quickly down Rue Montfaucon and turning left at the end into Rue Clement soon arrived at the door of his apartment building.

As he took off his coat and hung it behind the door, his thoughts returned to Janey and Adrienne. He wanted so much to be a part of their lives, but he knew that he would never rest until he had finally solved the mystery of what had happened to his wife Clemence after she left their apartment to visit a friend in 1942. Paris was a frightening place back then. The Germans had moved into the city on June 14th, 1940 and there was a general air of menace about the city. Lots of German troops patrolled the streets and gatherings of more than a few people were 'verboten'.

His thoughts turned to the letter that had arrived just before he left for London to visit Janey. He had placed an advert in Le Monde, asking anyone who had any clue about the whereabouts of his wife, either now or in the past, to contact him on a box number. He knew it was a very long shot but as he had been unable to get anywhere by going through the usual channels, he felt he had to try.

Three days later he had received a short letter. It was from a Madame Proust. The news it contained shocked him to the core. This lady had been arrested in the afternoon of the 16th July 1942, the very day that Clemence had left their apartment! His heart was hammering in his chest as he read on. Collaborating with the Germans, French gendarmes had rounded up thousands on that day and marched them through the streets to the Velodrome d'Hiver. Madame Proust said she had spent a couple of days inside the sports stadium with a young woman named Clemence. She didn't remember her second name. She said she would be willing to meet Francois and if he would bring a photo with him, she would probably be able to say if it was his wife Clemence.

At the bottom of the letter was a phone number. As he picked up the telephone and started to dial the number his hand was shaking. He had been searching for so long for his wife. Ten long years with no word and now, maybe this was the breakthrough he needed. A female voice answered.

'Hello, Madame Proust here, who is speaking please?'

'My name is Francois De Havilland. You answered my box number, about my wife, Clemence?' Francois replied tentatively.

'Hello Monsieur, I'm so glad you called, and I hope I will be able to help you, although I fear I won't have all the information you need to know.'

'Anything will be better than what I have right now Madame.'

He arranged to meet her the next day at the Café de Flore, in the Boulevard de St Germain-des-Pres.

He spent the evening selecting a photograph of Clemence that he judged to be a good likeness. The search awakened many memories of their all too short life together. They had been married just eighteen months when she went missing. They had met by chance at the Café de Flore in St Germain one summer day in 1939, fallen madly in love in the heady pre-war atmosphere of Paris and married a year later, just before the Germans marched into the city.

He spent a restless, mainly sleepless night. Images of Clemence drifted around his brain. What about Janey and Adrienne; could he contemplate not ever seeing them again if he did find Clemence? Was it possible that Clemence had been mistaken for a Jewish woman and been taken by the Germans? If that was true, could she possibly still be alive? Was he finally going to find her? Given the stories about what the Germans had done to the people in the camps, he realised it was more likely that she had perished at the hands of the Nazis. Very few people had survived the horrors of the death camps.

The morning was bright with a gentle breeze as he hurried along Rue Bonaparte towards the Café de Flore. It was mid-morning by the time he arrived and sat down at one of the tables on the boulevard. He had deliberately arrived early. From his vantage point on the corner of Rue Saint Benoit he could observe anyone approaching from either direction. Madame Proust had agreed to be carrying a copy of Le Monde so that he would recognise her. He had been here many times since it reopened after the war. It reminded him so much of Clemence and although it was sometimes painful, he also found it strangely comforting. One of the few links he still had to her.

Within a few minutes the waiter approached, and he ordered a café noir and then settled down to wait. After about fifteen minutes, at 10.30 precisely, he observed a middle aged lady approaching with a newspaper tucked under her arm. She was looking a little nervous and scanning the faces of his fellow customers. As he stood up, he caught her eye and she turned purposefully in his direction.

He judged her to be about forty-five, dressed neatly but not particularly fashionably. She wore no makeup, and her hair was pulled tightly back from her face. He would have called her severe-looking if it were not for the smile that broke out on her face as she walked towards him with her hand outstretched.

'Monsieur De Havilland, I presume?' she said lightly.

'Madame Proust,' Francois responded, 'Please, do sit down. Can I order you a coffee?'

'Yes, that would be nice. I'll have a café noir please.'

He beckoned the waiter and ordered her a coffee and another one for himself. Madame Proust seemed anxious to get down to business and immediately asked him if he had brought a photo. He pulled it out of the inside pocket of his jacket, saying that it was the best likeness he could find. It had been taken just a week or two before she disappeared. Madame Proust had perched her spectacles on her nose and scrutinised it carefully.

'It was a long time ago and we were only together for a couple of days, but they were terrifying days, not knowing what was going to happen next, and they are scorched in my memory,' she said.

She paused for a moment, then looked into Francois' eyes and announced, 'This is the young lady that I knew as Clemence.'

Francois sat back in his chair. His stomach churned and he blurted out

'Are you sure?'

'As sure as I can be after all these years. But yes, I am sure.' Madame Proust quickly assured him.

As the waiter appeared with their coffees, Francois took a moment to gather his thoughts.

He needed to know whatever she could tell him, and he said as much. His emotions were in turmoil. Maybe, just maybe he would soon find out what had happened to Clemence. He now realised that he had never stopped loving her since the day she disappeared.

'That day, 16th July 1942,' Madame Proust began, 'was the most horrific day of my life. We heard them coming up the street, shouting 'Vite, vite!' and banging on the doors.' She paused briefly, obviously upset at the memories it was evoking.

'Eventually they reached our door and started banging loudly,' she went on. 'There had been rumours that something like this was going to happen and I knew what it was as soon as I heard it and the fear gripped me there and then. I hesitated to answer the door, not knowing what to do. After a minute or so there was a loud crack as they burst in.

'Without waiting for me to grab anything apart from my two children, two armed policemen dragged me out of the door and told me to join the line of people walking down the street. I saw many of my neighbours but also many people I did not know. There were whole families, and they all looked terrified. The children clung to their mothers, many of them crying. The police kept urging us to go faster; shouting and brandishing their guns, occasionally poking someone in the back to keep them moving. There were many old people who were finding it hard to keep up, but the police showed little sympathy for them, shouting at them even more loudly.'

Francois, of course, had heard about this rounding up of the Jews at the time and had felt it was wrong, but had no idea how brutal it had been. At the time they were told that it was voluntary. The Jews wanted to leave Paris and the government was just helping them. Like everyone else he supposed he had believed what he wanted to believe and did and said nothing.

'I had no idea, I'm so sorry,' he felt impelled to say.

Madame Proust looked directly into his eyes but did not acknowledge his apology, which made him feel very uncomfortable. However, she went on,

'We had no idea where they were taking us. We seemed to be walking for ages but then we arrived at the Vélodrome d'Hiver. They herded us inside, and we couldn't believe what we were seeing as we entered the arena. There were thousands upon thousands of people already in there. None of them had any belongings apart from the odd bag or two. The noise was horrendous. People were shouting at the guards that ringed the arena, asking why they had been brought there. Children were crying, getting more and more distressed as the adults around them also began to break down in tears. We were 'encouraged' to join them, anyone hanging back being literally thrown into the central arena area.

'There were no seats in the central area and when we had wearied of standing, we sat on the floor. The minutes turned into hours and all the time more and more people were herded into the velodrome. People began to need to relieve themselves but weren't allowed to leave the area to find a lavatory. We had to designate areas that people could use but there was no privacy. Many people had little in the way of warm clothing and as the day wore on into evening, began to feel the cold, particularly the old and the children.'

Francois was feeling very uncomfortable and was anxious to bring the conversation back to Clemence.

As Madame Proust took a sip of her coffee he quickly and rather awkwardly interjected

'So how did you meet my wife?'

Madame Proust looked up sharply, and Francois noticed that her eyes were moist. Obviously these memories were very painful for her, but with a deep sigh she refocussed on the matter in hand.

'I had noticed a young woman, this young woman, protesting to one of the guards as we approached the velodrome, saying that there had been a terrible mistake and that she didn't belong there. It was to no avail. She turned and tried to run but was caught by the arm and thrown roughly to the floor. She scrambled to her feet and was pushed at gunpoint through the gate and into the arena.'

Francois was angry and shocked to the core. He couldn't believe that this had happened in Paris on a sunny July day in 1942, as he himself had been at home in their flat, cooking a meal for when his wife would return home. He had had some inkling about how the Jews had been treated but like many Frenchmen had chosen to put it to the back of his mind. Realising now that his own wife had been caught up in it all, he was angry and, yes, ashamed. Perhaps if he had had the courage to investigate, he may have been able to find her then and could have made the authorities release her.

His voice trembling with emotion he managed,

'I don't understand Madam. My wife wasn't Jewish.'

'Monsieur, not only Jews were taken that day. They also took anyone they suspected of working against the occupation. Maybe they thought she was involved in the underground.'

'But that is absurd!' he exclaimed, and then immediately apologised to Mdme Proust for his outburst.

'Please, monsieur,' she said, raising her hand in acknowledgement, 'I understand your anger. There were many injustices in those times, and not only perpetrated against we Jews. Who knows why they took your wife? It may simply have been a horrible case of mistaken identity.'

'Did you see her after that?'

Madame Proust nodded, 'I did. In fact, we spent two days and nights together in that dreadful place. Several times she tried to explain to the guards that she wasn't Jewish and that there had been some terrible mistake, but they would not listen and just shouted angrily at her, waving their guns in her face.

'You must understand that none of us knew what was going to happen to us. On the morning of the third day, there was suddenly a violent commotion as one of the captives went mad and charged at one of the guards. Others joined in, in the vain hope of overpowering them and escaping. Of course, it was completely hopeless. They were armed; we were not. They opened fire of course and many fell as they ran forwards. I had my two young children with me and my thoughts were all about trying to get them out of there. As all the attention of the guards were on the commotion at the other end of the arena, I saw my chance and escaped through the gate which they had temporarily left unattended. Of course, I had been unable to say goodbye to your wife and never saw her again. I am sorry, that is all I know.'

Francois sat for some moments, trying to absorb all that she had told him. To think of Clemence in that dreadful situation was tearing him apart. She must have been terrified. In all his imaginings of what had happened to her, he had never visualised anything like this. What was worse, he now knew that there was much more horror to come before he finally found out where she had gone and what had happened to her.

He dragged his attention back to the woman sitting in front of him. She was obviously very distressed at having to relive those moments in order to help him, and suddenly he was very grateful to her, and said as much.

Madame Proust nodded and smiled weakly.

'I only wish I could tell you more. All I do know, is that most of the people in that stadium were eventually sent to a transit camp in Beaune-la-Rolande, before they were eventually placed in the cattle trucks and sent to the East. I'm so sorry.'

This much, Francois had already known but this is something else that had been filed away somewhere at the back of his brain. Now he was being forced to retrieve the knowledge and understand that among those desperate people had been his own darling Clemence! At that moment he could find no words to express what he was feeling.

Once again, he thanked Madame Proust saying that he understood how difficult this must have been for her. She stood up and gracefully thanked him for the coffee before taking her leave.

Chapter 8

Francois and Clemence, 1953

Francois glanced at his wife sitting to his right. Even now he sometimes found it hard to realise that she was back in his life. She was still beautiful even though she looked older than her 35 years. He couldn't begin to imagine the horrors she had lived through during the ten years they had spent apart. In fact, he no longer tried. But even so, it was written in the lines of her face and the haunted look that sometimes, even now, crept into her eyes.

The guilt still surged through him whenever he thought about that day. The day she was taken. Somehow, he should have been able to find out what had happened to her. God knows he tried. Day after day he searched the streets of Paris. He spoke to everyone who knew her, but no-one had any clue as to where she had gone. Never in his wildest dreams did he imagine that she had been taken off the street. It literally just never occurred to him that such a thing could have happened. Of course, he now realised that once the Jews had been moved out of the Velodrome d'Hiver and taken to the transit camp and then to the East, he would have had no way of finding her. Within days she had no longer even been in Paris.

'Not long now,' he said to Clemence.

'That's good,' she replied, glancing across at him with a smile, 'it will be good to get home again.'

They had spent a couple of nights in Reims. It had been good to get out of Paris. At least, that's what he had felt, but Clemence seemed anxious the whole time, somehow unable to relax in the unfamiliar surroundings. Perhaps it had been a mistake but he was worried that she normally spent all her time in their apartment. She didn't seem to want to go anywhere or meet anyone else. He supposed it was because that's where she felt safe and secure.

He understood that it was still early days. He knew it would take time for her to adjust. He had understood that all too clearly, when he had first found her. She had been a shadow of his Clemence. She looked middle aged and under-nourished. Although there was a shadow of recognition in her eyes, it was clear that she hadn't known who he was at first. Over the subsequent days he had gradually re-awakened memories in her that had long been buried in an act of sheer survival.

For years her situation had dictated that all her energies had to be focussed on getting through each day. The things she had seen and endured had obliterated her emotions and with it, her memories. Life in the camps hardly justified the word. Surrounded by deprivation, death and torture, surviving to the next day was the most anyone could hope for.

When it was all over and she was released into the chaotic world of post-war Poland, it had been all she could do to go on surviving. With no money or memory of where she belonged she had been forced to beg, steal, borrow or worse, to stay alive. Eventually she had been placed in the Displaced Persons camp where he had found her. Finding her had, in itself, been a miracle. After he had spoken to Madame Proust he had begun to investigate where the people who had been in the Velome d'Hiver had been taken. This wasn't easy, but he'd been helped by a journalist who was investigating the role that the French police had played in the roundup. He learned that eventually they had mostly been taken to the Auschwitz camps in Poland. The journalist was able to check the list of names of people who hadn't survived but Clemence was not among them, which gave him some hope that maybe she was still alive somewhere. He had decided to go to Poland to try to pick up her trail. Using the Red Cross, who were helping concentration camp survivors to find their way home, he had found out that she was on the list of survivors living in Poland in the Displaced Persons camp near Lodz. That was where he found her, still recovering from the mental breakdown caused by what she had witnessed. She was still confused about her past, unsure who she was and where she belonged. She had no papers and knew only that she was called Clemence and because she spoke French it was assumed she had come from France.

As Francois patiently talked to her, little by little memories were rekindled and after a few weeks she was ready to accept that he was her husband and trusted him enough to return with him to Paris.

So here they were, a year later and outwardly they appeared to be just like any other couple, but Francois knew that the scars still went very deep and Clemence would probably never fully recover from the horrors she had endured. He had accepted that this would be his life from now on, caring for his wife who needed him more than ever. He also knew that he still loved her very much.

As for Janey and Adrienne, he had come to terms with losing them. He did feel guilty about abandoning them but comforted himself with the knowledge that he had at least made some provision for Adrienne in the form of an endowment trust which she could claim when she was twenty one. He had some money which had been left to him by his parents before the war. He'd had to be rather clandestine about it as he couldn't bring himself to tell Clemence that he had had a relationship resulting in the birth of a child. He had come up with the idea of the safety deposit box containing details of the trust fund and was rather pleased with the idea of having the numbers engraved on the bracelet which he sent anonymously to Janey. He would of course, make sure that Adrienne knew about the fund at some point, but that could wait for now.

He was musing about all this as he drove along the Riems to Paris road with Clemence, now dozing quietly in the passenger seat. As he glanced across to her he thought how beautiful she still was, in spite of the tell-tale lines around her eyes and mouth. He had never loved her more than he did at this moment. But precisely at that moment, fate took a hand as it so often does.

He never even saw the car emerging from the side road on the right, or the articulated lorry approaching from the opposite direction. He felt the impact from the side and the car being pushed across into the oncoming traffic and then, oblivion.

Chapter 9

Armand, Paris 1953

Armand strode purposefully down Rue Montfaucon and turning left at the end into Rue Clement soon found the address he had scribbled down earlier. It was dark and the street was empty as he opened the heavy glazed door and stepped into the hallway of the building. It was a typical Parisian apartment building, large, dark and with an air of faded grandeur. It had once been a grand house but had long since been divided up into apartments.

Apartment 31 he assumed would be on the third floor and so it turned out. The building was quiet apart from the distant sound of music emerging between the cracks around one of the doors on the first floor and voices raised apparently in anger from one on the second. Thankfully, no-one emerged from any of the doors, nor did he meet anyone as he climbed up to the third floor. Meeting someone now would never do.

He tried a couple of keys from the bunch in his hand before he found the one that fitted the lock. On entering the apartment, he found himself in a small hallway with three doors leading off. He opened the door on the right and locating the light switch, he could see that it was obviously the salon with a kitchen area through an archway at the far end. The room had a 'lived in' air about it. There were lots of books around, some china ornaments, and a couple of reading lamps with tasselled shades. The furniture was old, probably inherited from an earlier age and the carpet, although obviously of good quality had definitely seen better days.

There was a dark wood sideboard against one wall with several photographs carefully arranged along it. Picking one up, he could see that it was of the couple whose bodies he had dealt with that very day in the mortuary. So this was the man whose name he now bore. Francois De Havilland. He had to admit it did have quite a ring to it!

Replacing the photo, he sauntered around the apartment checking out each room. There was just one double bedroom and a bathroom off the entrance hall. The rooms were few, but they were large with high ceilings and tall windows. The salon window overlooked the street and the bedroom window looked out onto a central courtyard. In the kitchen he explored the cupboards and a small refrigerator. There was milk, cheese and eggs in the fridge and a couple of lagers. He helped himself to one of the beers and decided to make himself a cheese omelette for his supper. He felt rather at home here. It was a pity he couldn't stay around for a while, but within a few hours he would have to be gone and on the way to his new life.

As he sat eating his omelette, he pondered his next move. Things had gone well so far. Realising that those creatures were on his trail once more he had known that he had to find a way to shake them off. He needed to disappear, and fast! When the bodies had turned up in the mortuary this morning, he knew immediately that this was his chance. The man was about the same age, the colouring was right, and he looked about the same height and weight. He was on duty alone in the mortuary when the body bags were delivered, so no-one else had seen them. They were still fully dressed, and the man had his passport, driving license and keys in his jacket pockets. The woman had no papers or bag with her, or at least, there was nothing with the body. If her bag turned up later, it might present something of a problem for him. It was possible the police might eventually trace the driver through his car but he knew it would be two days or more before the mortuary attendants and therefore the police got around to dealing with the bodies, and he would be long gone by then.

When he had finished eating, he set about exploring the cupboards and drawers to find out everything he could about Francois De Havilland. After all, anything he could find would now become part of his own life story. The usual detritus of life turned up, bills, bank statements, and insurance policies, not that he would be able to claim any of them, he noted with regret. He briefly wondered if the woman had any life insurance policies he could claim on, but dismissed that as being too risky. What a pity, he thought.

Just when he thought that there wasn't anything else he could make use of, he found a box pushed right to the back of one of the sideboard drawers. It was secured with a small padlock which was easily dispensed with using a kitchen knife. Inside he found some letters from a woman signing herself Janey. Well, well, what had Francois been up to, he wondered. He read them all without the slightest compunction. After all, they were his letters now! There was also a photograph of the man holding a young child, presumably the girl Adrienne, who had been the subject of much of the correspondence.

As well as the letters there was a sealed envelope which he quickly tore open. Inside he found a key with a small label attached. The label had three numbers on it and further numbers had obviously been erased. With the key was a postcard explaining that it was the key to a safety deposit box. His heart beat a little faster. A safety deposit box! Well, that was a turn up. He might just have time to deal with that before he left Paris. In fact, as he read the rest of the postcard it became obvious that it wasn't going to be quite that simple. Although the card did explain where the box was being kept, it turned out that before it could be opened, he would need to find out what numbers had been erased. Excitement turned to anger as he realised that the only way he could find out what they were, would be to get hold of a bracelet that the stupid man had sent to this woman called Janey with the missing numbers engraved on it. Well, there was no way he could do anything about it right now, with the Hunters on his trail. He put the letters and the key back in the envelope with the postcard and stowed them all safely in the inside pocket of his jacket. One day, he would find a way!

He spent a further couple of hours searching the apartment for anything that he might find useful in his new life. He noted that the only photos were of the man and his wife. No children, apart that is, from the 'love child'. No older relatives. That's good, he thought. Doesn't look like either of them will be missed. This suited his plans perfectly. He filled a suitcase he had found on top of the wardrobe with some of the more decent clothes in the wardrobe, added a couple of expensive looking bits of china and some hallmarked silver ornaments he thought might raise a few francs.

At 12.30 am he drank the second can of lager, then put on a trench coat that had been hanging in the hall along with a trilby hat. Picking up the suitcase he pulled up the collar, pulled down the hat and opened the front door carefully, checking that no-one was about. Locking the door quietly, he quickly descended the stairs without encountering anyone, opened the front door and strode out into the night without a backward glance. He walked for about half a mile away from the apartment block before going down into the Metro at the Mobillon station.

He made his way over to Montmartre and to his own apartment. He took out the dead man's passport and his own and studied the photographs in each. If he shaved off his moustache and washed and restyled his hair, bringing it forward over his forehead, he felt he could make himself look pretty much like the dead man. When he had finished, he felt satisfied with the result. In any case, he didn't intend to actually be leaving France so he probably wouldn't even need to use the passport for years, if ever.

He had decided to travel down to the south; Marseilles, he thought. There were lots of cafés and restaurants needing staff, with the tourist industry picking up again. In any case, he would enjoy some sunshine after the dreariness of the Paris winter. When he was satisfied he had packed everything he could manage to carry in the two suitcases, he poured himself a whiskey and settled down in the armchair to await the arrival of the dawn.

As he drifted off to sleep he ran over once again the events of the day. Had he covered all his tracks sufficiently well to give himself time to disappear? He felt that he had. There was nothing on the bodies to lead them to the apartment in Rue Clement. Even if the authorities eventually found their way there, he was confident that there was nothing to connect him to them, apart from the fact that he had disappeared from the mortuary the same day the corpses had been delivered. As long as he kept a low profile in the future, he felt that he could happily become Francois D Havilland, safe once again from the clutches of the Hunters.

He arrived in Marseille on the morning of the 12th May 1953. Stepping down from the train he made his way out into the warm sunshine with a spring in his step. He had the amazing talent of leaving his history behind him. He prided himself in having no ability to feel guilt for anything. Even his part in the round up of the Jews, and the several 'unfortunate accidents' that had occurred. After all, he'd only been following orders. Of course, the Hunters didn't see it that way, but so long as he kept one step ahead of them, he could get on with his life. Taking this new identity without leaving any trace for them to find had been a masterstroke.

He had no trouble finding lodgings near the quayside and soon found work in one of the bars. He was pretty efficient, a good timekeeper, in fact an all-round reliable chap. He was paid by the day, cash in hand, so no records were submitted for tax purposes. Life was pretty good all in all. Of course, he kept himself to himself. There was no point risking detection by allowing anyone to get too close. He didn't mind that, he never felt he needed anyone else in his life. As long as he had money in his pocket and somewhere decent to live, that's all he required. He had always felt that relationships were a bit of an unnecessary burden. People always became possessive, expecting things, needing commitments he was never ready to give. So, he was what people might call 'a loner'.

Several years passed in this happy state and would have gone on indefinitely, then one day in 1962, he noticed someone standing across the street from his apartment who had not been there before. There was something about the way they were hanging around that made his nerves jangle. After a couple of days, he was convinced they were there to watch him, and he knew what that meant. The Hunters had found him again! He had to move fast if he was to escape their clutches once more. What was he to do? He had never earned much since he'd arrived in Marseilles and he hadn't risked using a bank account and so had no reserves. If he could get his hands on some money, he might be able to head east, maybe to Singapore or somewhere like that, where they perhaps wouldn't think of looking.

His thoughts returned to the Safety Deposit box in Paris. Was there any way he could entice that woman to bring him the bracelet with the missing numbers on it? He took out the letters taken from the flat in Rue Clement and read through them, looking for inspiration. He was delighted to read that the woman's father had disappeared from the Normandy beaches in 1940 and had never been declared dead. This gave him an idea. What if he was to write to the woman purportedly from someone near to her father, asking her to come to Paris to meet him but in the utmost secrecy, and bringing the bracelet with her as proof of her identity. It might work. What woman could resist following up news of a father previously supposed to be dead?

He hurriedly packed his suitcases that same evening and left the building by a back entrance, catching the early morning train to Paris. He booked into a pension and immediately wrote to the woman explaining that he had booked a room for her at L'Hotel Grande, Rue Mazarine and asking her to come to Paris. Of course, the plan depended on her being at the same address as she had been ten years previously, but he just had to hope that was the case, having no way of finding out one way or the other. After an anxious wait of three days of lying low, he finally received a short reply, stating that she was on her way to Paris and would book into the hotel he had suggested and would wait to hear from him once she had arrived.

Chapter 10

Janey, Paris, March 1962.

As Janey stepped down onto the platform at the Gare Du Nord, she was excited but also apprehensive. She was to a large extent moving into the unknown. Here she was in a strange country, about to arrange to meet someone she had never heard of before, on a quest to meet a father she could barely remember and had thought dead for decades. Put like that, she began to doubt the sanity of what she'd done, and without even telling anyone she was doing it. As she strode along the platform, still feeling bad that she'd left Marge a note to say she was going to Wiltshire to visit a friend, she determined that she should drop that postcard home as soon as possible to at least let them know where she actually was and to reassure them that she would be back soon.

As she passed through the ticket barrier, she took a moment to contemplate the scene. The concourse was huge. St Pancras was big enough, but this place was even bigger. It was busy with people hurrying to and fro or standing around obviously waiting to meet someone. She always enjoyed railway stations. They seemed to carry a delicious air of expectation and heightened emotion. They were places full of the little one act plays of life. Couples embracing, someone rushing to catch a train, families with suitcases and little children, mum and dad trying to keep everyone together and moving in one direction. This one was particularly exciting. Familiar, but at the same time very different. The smell was of French cigarettes mingled with diesel from the trains and an all pervasive odour of garlic. The whole mix was unlike anything she had smelt before. Not unpleasant, just different. People were chatting to each other, in French, of course. She did have some French, learned in school, but had never had occasion to use it since. There seemed to be an excessive use of hand gestures and the voices were rising and falling in unfamiliar cadences.

She looked around for an information office so that she could buy a map of the city, and spotting a sign which read Visitors Bureau, headed for it. With some difficulty and not a little embarrassment she managed to explain to the person behind the desk that she needed a map to locate Rue Mazarine. Emerging with a Paris guide and Metro map, she made her way to a coffee bar on the concourse, ordered a café noir and settled down at a table to study her next move. It didn't actually look too far away, and she thought that rather than negotiating the Metro, it might be rather good to walk, so that she could soak up the Parisian atmosphere and get her bearings at the same time.

Having worked out her route, she finished her coffee, picked up her belongings and strode out into a sunny Paris afternoon. She walked along Rue de Mauberge under the structure which formed a footbridge between the buildings on each side of the street. Checking her map as she came to the junction of several roads, she turned left into the Rue de Magenta which was a pleasantly broad and tree lined boulevard. The first thing that struck her was the apparently random movements of the traffic. Quite unlike the orderly procession of vehicles moving sedately around London. Actually, it rather added to the excitement. It all seemed completely unpredictable and yet, it worked, and they all kept moving, somehow avoiding collisions.

She was also rather surprised to see armed soldiers standing on some of the street corners, until she remembered that there had been trouble recently with something called the OAS. She wasn't really sure about the details but believed it was something to do with Algeria, a French colony, demanding their independence. She had to admit it was rather unsettling. After a few hundred meters she approached a church on her left, and consulting the map once more, she crossed the boulevard and took a right turn into Boulevard de Strasbourg. She concluded that she needed to follow this for a couple of kilometres, almost as far as the Seine. She now relaxed into her walk, enjoying the nineteenth century architecture of the buildings, many with wrought iron balustrades at the windows, which reminded her of the architectural career she had dreamed of, but in the end circumstances hadn't allowed her to follow, but her love of the subject had always persisted. There were several shops along the way, some of them with awnings out to protect their goods from the glare of the sun. Every so often she would pass a grating in the pavement when that unique smell of the Paris Metro, mainly garlic, and diesel fumes, would fill her nostrils.

As Janey walked, her mind drifted back to the matter in hand, reminding her that she needed to buy a postcard to send home to Marge. She stopped at a marchand de journeaux, chose a card with several views of Paris and paid at the counter. She determined to write and post it as soon as she could. She would feel better when Marge was more fully in the picture. Continuing along the boulevard she approached a tall, white, and beautiful tower which looked as if it should have had a church attached to it. Consulting the map, she could see that this was the Tour Saint Jacques and that she now needed to turn left in front of it into the Rue de Rivoli and then take a right, turning towards the river and the Pont Notre Dame. As she emerged from between the buildings onto the bridge, she immediately saw the familiar wonderful outline of Notre Dame Cathedral over to her left on the other side of the Seine. She knew that the Hotel Grande, where she was staying was now no more than ten minutes away, on the south side of the river. Glancing at her watch she could see it was two-thirty. She felt she had plenty of time before she needed to check in to the hotel and decided to explore the Isle de la Cite, with its famous flower and bird markets. It didn't disappoint. There were caged birds of all kinds on sale and birdsong filled the air as she approached the market. As she had expected it was busy here. The French certainly love their caged birds, she mused. The variety of flowers on display was amazing too, and they were doing good trade.

It suddenly occurred to her that she hadn't eaten since breakfast and she spotted a pavement café across the street. Janey sat down at one of the outside tables and when the waiter approached, ordered a coffee and a pastry. She decided it would be a good time to write that postcard to Marge, obviously not giving too much away until she had contacted the person who had sent her the letter. She did tell Marge that she was in Paris and would be home soon, mentioning that she would be meeting someone who would give her the answers she needed. She hoped Marge wouldn't worry too much, and once she was home, she would explain everything. She would need to find somewhere to buy a stamp for the card and made a mental note to ask at the hotel where the nearest post office was. In the meantime, she popped it into her handbag.

Picking up her belongings, she settled the bill and

using the map once more made her way to Rue Mazarine, quickly locating number forty, euphemistically called L'Hotel Grande. It was obviously nothing of the kind but as she entered it seemed clean enough and there was a pleasant woman on the desk. Janey told the woman that a reservation had been booked for her. Checking in the book in front of her the woman nodded and lifted a room key from the array on the wall behind her. She gave Janey the key and explained that the room was on the second floor, at the far end of the landing. The bathroom was a shared one and was two doors along from room 210. Janey asked the woman whether there had been any messages left for her but apparently there was nothing. This unnerved her slightly. She had come a long way to see this stranger but had no idea when or where she would actually meet him (or indeed, her) until she was contacted. Once again, she wondered if coming here was entirely wise; but it was too late now, to think about that.

She let herself into the room which was sparsely but adequately furnished with a double bed, a small wardrobe, a dressing table with a chair and in one corner a sink with a mirror over it. Not exactly the height of luxury she thought, but it will do. She wasn't sure how long she would need to be here. It occurred to her that she should have checked with the concierge how long the room was booked for. She also made a mental note to ask about a post office. Kicking off her shoes she lay on the bed, deciding what to do next. There was no phone in the room so presumably a message would be left with the concierge telling her where and when to meet the mysterious stranger, so she would just need to check regularly, to see whether anything had arrived. She took out the letter she'd received just three days ago and read it again for the umpteenth time. It read,

Miss Grainger,

You don't know me, but I have been asked by your father to arrange for you to come to Paris as he wants to see you. He says he is aware this may come as something of a shock as he hasn't been in a position to contact you for many years. Now he is desperate to see you. Because of his current precarious circumstances it will be necessary to meet me first, and so that I can be sure of your identity, he asks that you bring the bracelet he sent to your mother some years ago. You will be booked into L'Hotel Grande on the Rue de Mazarine from Friday next. Once you arrive please wait for a message from me when I will let you know when and where to meet me. Please don't let your father down, he is relying on you. Please tell absolutely no-one about this, your father's life may depend on absolute secrecy.

Au-revoir until we meet in Paris.

AD

There was a return address on the back of the envelope, and she had written a reply, telling them that she was on her way to Paris, and had dropped it into a post box on her way to the station that morning.

Folding the letter and placing it back in the envelope, she got up and decided to get ready for the 'summons', whenever it should arrive.

She took herself along to the rather functional bathroom to freshen up, then changed into a pair of grey slacks and a yellow blouse that tied in a knot at her waste. She felt it was quite fashionable. Brushing her hair and applying some lipstick she was pleased enough with the overall result as she glanced in the dressing table mirror. Deciding to go out to find something to eat, she picked up her coat and handbag and trotted downstairs, stopping to ask the concierge whether any message had yet arrived for her.

Nothing had been delivered for her so stepping into the street she looked around to see if there were any restaurants in the vicinity. She spotted one on the corner of the next street and strode purposefully towards it. She settled down at a table near the window and when the waiter arrived, she ordered a seafood salad.

After taking a stroll around the Ile de La Cite, soaking up the atmosphere and admiring the Gothic architecture of Notre Dame, she returned to her hotel, and after checking that there was still no message, decided on an early night.

The next morning, as soon as she had showered and dressed, Janey quickly went down to reception to check whether any messages had arrived. To her surprise, the concierge said 'Ah oui Madame,' and handed her an envelope addressed to Miss J. Grainger. She thanked the woman and even though she was desperate to open it, stuffed it into her bag until she could find somewhere more private to read it.

Once settled in a café over the road, Janey ordered breakfast before taking the envelope the concierge had given her out of her bag. She quickly tore it open and found a short note inside. All it said was.

'Meet me at 7.30 tonight in the Square de Vert-Gallant, on the Ile de la Cite. Don't forget to bring the bracelet' AD.

It was in the same hand as the letter, so Janey had to assume it was genuine, but had to admit it was all very clandestine. No mention of her father this time, and he (or she) seemed awfully keen to have sight of that bracelet, which made her rather nervous to say the least. Still, she had come this far and would have to see it through. Delving into her bag she pulled out the small box containing the bracelet. Opening it she inspected the bracelet as she had done countless times since receiving the first letter. It was spectacularly unremarkable. Just a plain silver band, its only decoration being the three numbers 739, engraved on the inside of it. She had always assumed this must be a maker's code or an assay mark showing the grade of silver used to make it. Now it seemed that the bracelet was to identify her, so perhaps that's what the numbers were for after all, as there were no other distinguishing features that she could see. Putting the message and the bracelet safely in her handbag, she paid the bill and stepped out into the cool morning air. So, this was it, tonight she would find out what this was all about. Although not really in the mood for sightseeing, with several hours to fill before the meeting, she thought she may as well see a bit of Paris while she was here. She took the metro to Montmartre to visit the magnificent Sacre Coeur, which impressed her greatly, given her long standing passion for architecture.

Chapter 11

The Meeting, Paris, March 12th 1962

Seven o'clock found Janey making her way toward Pont Neuf. She was a little early, but that was all to the good. She thought she would find somewhere to hide, from where she could survey the meeting point and assess the situation when 7.30pm arrived. At least then, she would be able to see who had written the letter and the note. She also felt that this way she could maintain some control over events, although in reality she knew that he (or she) still held all the cards until she had found out where her father was.

She walked, slowly and carefully now. It was getting rather darker than she would have liked as she prepared to meet a perfect stranger, but it was too late to worry about that now. As she crossed the bridge, she noticed the sign to the Square du-Vert-Gallant but as she approached, she was dismayed to see that she had to descend a steep staircase to access the park where she was meant to meet this AD, whoever he was. This all seemed very clandestine, but she supposed this was because of the need for secrecy surrounding her father. As she stepped into the park, she saw that it was quite small, and shaped like the prow of a ship.

Walking towards the end of the park, she noticed the Eiffel Tower in the distance against the night sky. Not sure exactly where the meeting point was to be and bearing in mind that she wanted to have sight of the person in advance, she chose to stand behind some bushes over to the left of the park. From there, she could observe the bottom of the staircase, which was about fifty yards away, whilst remaining out of sight herself. At seven thirty precisely, she saw a tall, dark man walking along the Pont Neuf above the park. In the streetlights there was something rather familiar about him. Oh my God, she thought, it can't be! Can it? She was almost convinced it was Francois! As he emerged from the staircase, into the area lit by a lamp, she was sure it was him and stepping out from her hiding place, she strode, almost running, towards the man. Her heart was racing, sure, for a few moments that it was indeed her ex-lover, the father of her child! She even called out his name, before being hit by crushing disappointment. Although this man did look like Francois, it wasn't him! With shock, she now realised that she had exposed herself before she'd had time to make any kind of assessment of the situation.

He was now striding towards her, with his hand outstretched in greeting.

'You must be Miss Grainger,' he said, rather formally.

He looked to be about forty as far as she could see in the half light. He was quite tall with slicked back black hair. Whether it was the situation or not, he did cut a rather sinister figure and Janey was immediately nervous of what might follow. She was feeling, even more than before, that coming here wasn't the best idea she'd ever had. He asked her whether she had the bracelet.

The bracelet again, she thought! But the bracelet wasn't the reason she was here, was it? She was here to meet her father and said as much.

'All in good time,' he retorted. 'First, show me the bracelet!'

She didn't much care for his tone. She was beginning to get angry now, feeling that he was going to welch on the agreement. She replied sharply.

'Take me to my Dad first, and I'll give him the bracelet.'

'That's not how it works, little lady,' he replied with a sneer, and tried to grab her handbag.

In a flash, Janey now realised that the whole thing had been about getting the bracelet to Paris. For what reason, she couldn't guess and didn't have time to think about. He was pulling at her bag strap, trying to wrestle it from her. As he snatched it, she suddenly lost her grip and tumbled backwards. As she fell, her head hit the railings and she slid down to the pavement, unconscious. Francois saw his chance. After looking around to make sure there was no-one about, he quickly picked up Janey's apparently lifeless body and tipped it over the low railings onto the parapet and then into the fast-flowing waters of the River Seine.

The instant Janey hit the water, the shock of it brought her round and she realised with horror that she was in the water and fighting for her life against the powerful currents swirling around the island. Twice she managed to pull herself back up for air, but the third time, the current was just too strong, and she was sucked down once more into the blackness. In that instant, she realised that no-one would ever know what had happened to her – the postcard was still in her handbag, waiting for its stamp! Adrienne's sweet face was the last thing she saw as the blackness closed in around her.

Francois picked up the handbag and strode off without a backward glance. Janey had just been 'collateral damage' in his quest to get his hands on whatever was inside that safety deposit box. He had the numbers, and nothing could stop him now. He would be at the bank first thing in the morning to claim his prize! After he had placed the bracelet, the letter, and the note he had written, safely in his jacket pocket, he realised he must get rid of the woman's handbag. He first checked that her passport wasn't in it, took out her purse, and after getting well away from the scene of her demise, threw the handbag into some bushes. He never even noticed the postcard tucked inside the side pocket of the bag. As far as he was concerned, that was that. Now he would have the means to escape the Hunters once and for all.

First of all he realised that it might be wise to visit her hotel room to remove all trace of her so that if someone should come looking for her, they would reach a dead end. It was about eleven o'clock by the time he judged it would be quiet enough to slip into the hotel unnoticed. The concierge was busy talking on the telephone and scrutinising the book on the desk and he managed to walk unnoticed to the flight of stairs round the corner. He quickly located the room he had booked for her and using his trusty penknife managed to unlock the door. He threw all of Janey's belongings into her holdall. Her passport and train tickets which he found in the drawer next to the bed he tucked into his jacket pocket so that he could dispose of them safely later. Checking around to make sure there was nothing else he quietly left the room. As luck would have it the concierge was dealing with a noisy guest who had had a little too much to drink and it wasn't difficult to slip past without being noticed. He disposed of the holdall in a rubbish bin.

Next morning, in his hotel room, he tore the pages out of the passport and ripped them into shreds along with the train tickets. He left the cheap guesthouse he had been staying in while waiting for the bracelet to arrive and made his way to the bank designated on the postcard he had found in Francois' apartment, explaining about the safety deposit box. On his way he threw the pieces of the passport and tickets into the Seine.

With his 'passport' and the six numbers he had no problem gaining access to the secure room in the basement where he assumed, the box would be brought to him to open. The bank official who had escorted him to the room left, and returned some minutes later with the box, laid it in front of him and handed him the key. The official then left the room while he examined the contents.

He had imagined many times what might be contained in the box. Gold, jewellery maybe? Stocks and share certificates perhaps? What he actually found, shocked, and angered him. It wasn't anything that he could immediately turn into cash. It was a letter from an investments and insurance company, setting out the details of an endowment trust due to mature in 1971, which was bad enough, but even worse than that from his point of view, it was not in his 'name' but in the name of Adrienne Grainger, the love child of that woman and the man from whom he had stolen his identity all those years ago. He took the letter and placing it in his jacket pocket along with his passport, angrily slammed the lid shut and rang the bell for the attendant to return and allow him to leave.

So, he would have to wait at least another nine years before he would have a chance of turning this piece of paper into a sizeable sum of money, which by then could be worth over half a million francs! Even then, he could only do it with the help, willing or not, of the girl, Adrienne. OK then, time for plan B. He would make his way to the port city of Le Havre and find work on one of the many merchant steamers which criss-crossed the globe and let the ocean take him to a place where he could quietly disappear again, away from the prying eyes of the Hunters. In nine years' time he would find a way to get his hands on the money. He would look on it as his retirement fund!

Chapter 12

Wembley 11th March 1962

Marge had arrived home from work at about 4 o'clock that afternoon. Adrienne was already home from school and was swinging on the front gate as she strode up the street.

'Mum not home yet?' Marge asked her breezily.

'Not yet Aunty,' Adrienne replied. 'I hope she hurries up; I was hoping we could go to the library after tea today and they close at seven.'

'I'm sure she won't be long,' Marge reassured her as she walked up the path to the front door.

Janey had lived with Marge since her mother, Beatrice, Marge's sister had died of a heart attack. It had made sense for Marge and Beatrice to share the house which had, in fact, always been the family home. Beatrice had stayed there even when she married Janey's dad Fred before the war. They'd hardly had any time together as Fred had been left on the Dunkirk beaches, presumed dead, although this was never confirmed. When Beatrice died, it just made sense for Janey and her Aunt Marge to stay together. Later, when Adrienne came along, Marge was able to help Janey with childcare and they shared living costs.

After she had freshened up, Marge busied herself preparing their evening meal. A nice green salad with new potatoes and some roast ham. By five the meal was on the table waiting for Janey to arrive. It was still there at six when Marge decided they had better start without her. Adrienne was most upset because now she wouldn't have time to visit the library, it would have to wait until tomorrow.

It wasn't like Janey not to let her know if she would be working late and this almost never happened on a Friday night. If anything, she would have been early on Fridays. Janey worked in the local chemist's shop in the high street, serving behind the counter and stocking the shelves and so on. The shop closed at six, so before she ate her meal, Marge decided to give the manager a ring, to find out what time Janey had left.

She was shocked to hear that Janey hadn't been to work at all that day. What on earth was going on, Marge wondered. It was then that she noticed a white envelope tucked underneath the telephone. It was addressed to her and it was in Janey's handwriting. She tore it open and what she read astonished her and at the same time made her rather angry. It read:

Dear Marge,

Sorry to land this on you but could you look after Adrienne for a few days. I got a letter this morning from a friend down in Wiltshire – I don't think it's anyone you would know just an old school friend. Anyway, she's very ill and wants to see me urgently, so I've packed a few things and will be home as soon as I can.

Love Janey x

Well! That's a bit much, she thought. Fancy dropping everything just like that. It wasn't that she minded looking after Adrienne, in fact it was always good fun to be with her, just the two of them. Just wait until she gets back, she thought, I'll be giving her a piece of my mind, to be sure!

Adrienne was also rather put out and couldn't understand why her mum would have gone away, even though it was only for a day or two, without even saying goodbye. Anyway, she was past the age of bursting into tears whenever things didn't go quite the way she'd planned, so she just shrugged her shoulders and started thinking about what she and Marge might do over the next day or two. In fact, they had a lovely weekend. On the Saturday they visited the library so that they could change their library books. They spent the afternoon down by the river, reading and eating ice-cream in the sunshine. Sunday morning was spent tidying the garden, and then Adrienne asked if her friend Natalie could come round for the afternoon.

Marge was still pretty cross with Janey for just taking off like that, but her anger turned to worry as the days passed. Monday, Tuesday, Wednesday came and went with no word from Janey. Adrienne was getting more and more upset. By Thursday night she couldn't sleep, and Marge determined to contact the police the next day as she herself had no way of finding out where Janey was. She had looked through Janey's papers and address books but could find no one with a Wiltshire address. The next day she walked into the police station to report her as a 'missing person'. Because Janey had left a note saying where she had gone, the surly sergeant on duty refused to take it seriously. Even though Marge explained that she had found no record of any of Janey's associates living in Wiltshire, he merely said,

'Well, madam, your niece obviously knew exactly where she was going.' And Marge could hardly argue with the logic of that as the note was definitely in Janey's handwriting.

It was a further two weeks before Marge was able to convince the local constabulary that something was badly wrong and she, and they, had been forced to the conclusion that Janey was indeed 'a missing person'. The police now placed posters at the railway station and the bus terminus which carried a picture of Janey and the words 'Missing; if you have seen this lady, please contact Wembley Police Station'. To be truthful there wasn't much more they could do. In the event, no one ever came forward to say that she had been sighted. Weeks turned into months, then into years. Adrienne suffered badly for the first few months, but eventually seemed to accept the situation and just got on with her life.

She was a bright girl and Janey had always encouraged her to work hard at school and inspired her to aim high in whatever she did. Of course, losing her mum at such a young age and the fact that she had no idea why, had its effect on her. She became quite introverted and where before she had found it easy to make friends, now she was always wary of new relationships. She found it difficult to trust people, as the one person who meant most to her had just disappeared without so much as a goodbye. In spite of that, she did do well at school and gained a place at teacher training college. Marge did her best to fill Janey's shoes but of course there was no substitute for the very close relationship mother and daughter had forged over the years.

It was in February 1972, almost ten years after Janey's disappearance that a letter turned up addressed to Marge. Inside was a postcard of Paris. Turning it over, Marge was astonished to see that it was written and signed by Janey and dated the day she had disappeared from their lives. The note read.

11th March 1962

Marge,

I'm sorry I had to lie to you in my note. In fact, I wanted to let you know I'm actually here in Paris at L'Hotel Grande, Rue Mazarine, but I'm alright. I hope you and Adrienne are OK. I'm sorry I had to leave without telling you everything, but I know it was for the best and I'll explain it all when I get back. I'm meeting some-

one tonight who will give me the answers I need and hopefully, I'll be home next week.

Love Janey.

Marge was shocked to the core. Ten years ago, Janey had gone to Paris, not Wiltshire! And she had expected to be back home within days. Something terrible must have happened to stop her coming home. She would never have abandoned Adrienne. Marge knew that with certainty. So what now? Along with the postcard from Janey was a handwritten note from someone called Gabrielle. It said that some years ago she had been walking through a small park in Paris and had noticed a handbag in the bushes. She had picked it up and taken it home as it looked quite new and good quality, thinking there might be something inside to say who had lost it. As there hadn't been anything to identify the owner she had put it into the cupboard along with her own handbags. It wasn't until recently that she had taken it out, thinking she might like to use it. To her surprise, tucked down the side pocket she had found the enclosed postcard. It had been addressed but not stamped but Gabrielle had though that it might be of importance to the addressee and had decided to send it on. She hoped that the delay in sending it hadn't caused any problems for anyone. There was no return address or even a surname, so Marge wasn't able to reply.

Although so much time had passed since Janey had disappeared, Marge knew she would have to try to find out what had happened to her. She decided not to mention it to Adrienne just yet. She'd been through enough and until she had some positive news, she thought it best not to discuss it with her. She determined to hire a private detective agency to see if they could find out anything for her. In the meantime, she tucked the postcard away inside her other papers in the black file on top of her wardrobe for safety. Of course, she never got the chance to pursue the matter, as within less than a week, she was dead.

Chapter 13

Paris, 1972

After leaving Paris in 1962 Armand had finally fetched up in Singapore having worked his passage as a deck hand on the steamship Straat Johore. It was a bustling and growing city and signing off the ship, he had no problem finding work. There, he settled down for the next ten years. He did pretty well for himself in Singapore, taking a job with an import agency and working his way up to become a warehouse manager. He had almost forgotten about Adrienne and her endowment.

By chance, his interest was about to be re-awakened when he picked up an English newspaper one day on the quayside, no doubt left by a British tourist hurrying to catch his cruise ship. Perusing the inside pages, he noticed an article about a hit and run accident. As he read on, he saw that the name of the deceased was Marjorie Whitehead and that the accident had been witnessed by her niece Adrienne Grainger! He recognised the name immediately, and the woman who had been killed must be the Marge who was mentioned in the letters he'd found at the man's apartment all those years ago. Most likely then, this would be the person who had brought up the girl since her mother's unfortunate 'accident' and also, possibly the only person who would have met and known the real Francois. He also realised that the girl, Adrienne, would now be a woman and would be twenty-two, old enough to claim the endowment money from the insurance company.

All he needed to do now was to figure out a detailed plan as to how he could get his hands on the money. He decided that the girl would probably be feeling quite vulnerable right at this moment, and that he may as well make the most of that. It was time for Adrienne to meet her long-lost daddy!

He had to act fast. He had some leave due and immediately booked a flight to England for the next day. Once there, he would find out from the local newspaper or funeral directors when the funeral was to take place. She would be at her most vulnerable at that point he felt, and that would give him his chance.

Now, as he sat outside the Café de Flore waiting for Adrienne to join him, he was thinking that it had worked out rather well. It had been easier than he expected to convince the girl that he was her father. His judgement about her vulnerability had proved correct. Of course, he had been somewhat shaken when she told him about the postcard, until he realised that in fact, he could turn it to his advantage. It gave him the perfect excuse to be with her in Paris. He hadn't quite figured out yet how he was going to use her to claim the endowment money, but now that she was determined to find out what had happened to her mother, he could at least be by her side, able to guide events if need be.

After arriving at the Gard Du Nord the previous day Adrienne had caught a taxi, asking the driver to take her to L'Hotel Rivoli which was the one recommended by Francois and which she had booked into for two weeks, using her local travel agent back home. She hoped that would be long enough to do what she had to do. She was excited to be in Paris, not least because it was the last place she knew for certain her mother had been before she disappeared. She was determined to find out what had happened to her. Could there even be a chance she was still alive!?

The taxi pulled up in front of a small hotel which, frankly, looked as if it had seen better days. It certainly wasn't the Ritz, she thought. Still, she supposed it would serve the purpose of providing her with a base in the centre of the city from where she could conduct her enquiries. As it happened the hotel looked better on the inside than first impressions had suggested. The concierge was pleasant enough and wished her a good stay as she handed her the room key. The room itself wasn't large, but it did have a small en-suite bathroom and it was all very clean and tidy, so she was happy enough with it.

Unpacking her case, she set out the contents of her toilet bag in the small en-suite bathroom. She ordered coffee and croissants from room service, then freshened up and changed into a pair of slacks and blue jumper. Eager to get started on her quest she had rung the number Francois had given her and asked the receptionist to put her through to his room. He had seemed very happy to hear from her and arranged to meet her that evening at the Café de Flore, on Boulevard St Germain-des-Pres, to discuss how they might begin to search for clues as to what had happened to her mother. He had given her directions to the café and said he was looking forward to seeing her again. She checked her handbag to make sure she had the postcard and also a picture of her mother taken just before she disappeared. She spent a moment looking at the photo and whispered softly 'Not long now Mum', before tucking it back into her handbag.

Adrienne had twenty minutes or so before she was to meet Francois, and checking the map of the city the travel agent had given her, decided to walk towards the Pont Neuf at the western end of the Ile de la Cite, which, she decided, would be taking her in the general direction of the Café de Flore. She picked up her bag and slung it over her shoulder, and after handing her room key in at the reception desk, stepped out into the street. She turned left towards the Seine, noticing the gothic bulk of Notre Dame that was over to her left. Her route took her along the river to the right until she came to the Pont Neuf. As she crossed the bridge, she made a mental note to visit the cathedral before leaving Paris. She too had a love of architecture, inherited, she supposed, from her mother.

Reaching the Ile de La Cite, she noticed a small triangular park to the right, some metres below the road. The notice said 'Square du Vert-Gallant. She stopped and looked down into the park. It was shaped like the prow of a ship and the waters of the Seine flowed quickly past on either side Staring down at the water, with its swirling currents, she suddenly felt very cold and shivered, thinking that anyone falling in at this spot would be quickly swept away. Now where on earth did that thought come from, she wondered. After a few moments she glanced at her watch and saw that she was due to meet Francois in about ten minutes and still had a fair way to walk, then turned and set off at a brisk pace.

Frequently consulting her map, she made her way inexorably towards their meeting point. Her nerves began to jangle at the prospect of meeting Francois again. The thought of him always engendered mixed emotions in her. There was the excitement of finding she had a father, something she had never imagined, but she would have loved to believe they could have a future together. Yet there were too many things that didn't feel right. Him turning up out of the blue at the funeral; his having no idea why Janey had wanted to see him; how had she known he was even in Paris? Well, she may soon have answers to some of these questions at least. Taking a final left turn into Rue Saint Benoit, she could see the Café Flore at the end of the street. She saw him immediately, sitting at a table at the outer edge of the seating area, obviously surveying the approaches so as not to miss her appearance. He saw her and raised a hand in recognition.

Chapter 14

Francois and Adrienne Meet in Paris

Francois greeted her with the two customary kisses enjoyed in those parts, although the greeting wasn't enjoyed by Adrienne. Far too familiar, she thought. She quickly stepped back and then sat down at the table in the chair opposite him. She wasn't yet ready to allow him to get too close to her.

'It's lovely to see you again,' he said, with apparent warmth.

'Err, yes, you too,' she replied rather stiffly and a little too quickly.

'What can I get you?' he asked, 'Are you hungry?'

'Not very,' she lied. Actually she was famished but for some reason didn't particularly want this to turn into a shared meal.

'Well, just a snack then,' and called the waiter across, ordering some sandwiches and a mixed salad.

'So, where to start then?' he asked tentatively.

'Well, first of all, is this the café where you arranged to meet mum?' Adrienne responded.

'No, actually it isn't far from here, just around the corner in fact. We can go there afterwards although I'm not really sure how much help that would be, as of course, your mother never actually turned up there that evening.'

'Still, I would like to see it if you don't mind,' she insisted.

'Of course, we'll go round there after we've eaten.'

'The next thing I would like to do is visit the hotel where she was staying.'

Francois looked a little taken aback at this.

'You mean, you know where she was staying?' he asked sharply.

The slight alarm in his tone of voice wasn't lost on Adrienne. Now, why should that bother him, she thought.

'Oh, didn't I mention that? It was written on the postcard.' she replied, as she took the postcard out of her bag and handed it to him.

As he looked at the postcard his expression was not at all what she had expected. Surely, confronted with the last known correspondence from someone who had once meant so much to him should have elicited some emotion? None was apparent. She found this rather disconcerting. After all, it was an emotional message from her mother to a family who had no idea where she was. His reaction, or lack of it, was definitely odd.

'L'Hotel Grande,' he read the name slowly out loud. 'Well, if I had known that at the time, I could have gone there to try to find her, but of course I didn't know it.'

There followed a rather awkward silence during which *Francois* seemed deep in thought while they continued to eat their meal. Adrienne would have loved to question him further about his thoughts on why Janey had come to Paris and what she might have wanted to see him about. However, his demeanour was rather 'closed' and to be honest she didn't know where to start.

When they had finished eating, he called the waiter over and asked for the bill without asking Adrienne whether she would like anything else. She reminded him that he was going to show her where he had been supposed to meet Janey, and after he'd settled the bill, they made their way down Rue Benoit to a little café she'd noticed on her way to meet him earlier. He was right, of course, this place would yield no clues as Janey had never actually turned up that day. She was now pinning all her hopes on L'Hotel Grande. He offered to walk her back to her hotel, but she graciously declined, as she really needed to be alone, to sort out the myriad thoughts and feelings running through her head.

They said goodnight, arranging to meet near L'Hotel Grande in the morning. As she walked along towards the Ile de la Cite and Notre Dame cathedral, she was mulling over *Francois*' change in attitude when she had mentioned L'Hotel Grande and also, his lack of emotional response when he'd read the postcard worried her. This didn't seem like the response which she would have expected from someone who had once been close to Janey, particularly as she was the mother of his long-lost child, who was sitting across the table from him at that very moment.

She began thinking about her mother and how she may have walked these very streets. What on earth had brought her to Paris? Was it really to see *Francois*? If it was, why all the secrecy? He said he hadn't asked her to go there and insisted that he didn't know why she had. So why? Surely, she wouldn't have taken off like that unless she had a sound reason for doing so. Like, for example, an invitation to meet someone and as he had admitted that she had arranged to meet him, then surely there's a good chance it was he who had invited her. And yet he denies this. It's all very confusing.

She checked in to her hotel and was grateful to flop into the surprisingly comfortable bed. In fact, she had a restless night, rather overtired from the journey and the excitement and the apprehension she had been feeling since leaving home that morning.

The next day dawned bright and warm and after taking a shower Adrienne dressed quickly in a woollen skirt and jumper, and flat sling back sandals for comfort, in case there would be a lot of walking around.

She had arranged to meet *Francois* at nine o'clock for coffee and croissants at the café around the corner from L'Hotel Grande in Rue Mazarine. It was about a twenty minute walk away, but she walked briskly and arrived early. She ordered herself a coffee au lait and a pain au chocolat. At nine o'clock precisely she saw *Francois* striding down the street. He was casually dressed in slacks and a brightly coloured cotton shirt and brown jacket. He is rather good looking, she thought, for one moment allowing herself to believe that he was the kind of dad she would like to have had, if he'd been around.

To her slight annoyance he greeted her with the usual two kisses and light embrace. She understood it was the French way, but it still seemed far too familiar for her taste. He ordered himself a coffee and croissants, asking her if she'd like anything else. She asked for another coffee.

'Lovely morning,' he said cheerfully.

'It certainly is,' she replied brightly, then after the waiter had brought their order, she jumped straight into the business of the day.

'So, have you been to L'Hotel Grande before?' she asked him tentatively.

'I don't think so,' he replied.

Well, she thought, doesn't he know whether he has or he hasn't? More grounds for suspicion! Nothing's ever straightforward with him, she thought.

'I hope you aren't getting your hopes up too high,

Adrienne.' he said suddenly, 'It is ten years ago and the staff have probably changed since then.'

'I know,' Adrianne replied impatiently, 'but we have to start somewhere and it's the only clue I have.'

They turned the corner into Rue Mazarine and there in front of them was the Hotel Grande, although Adrienne thought that it didn't actually look very grand.

They walked up the couple of steps to the glazed door and *Francois* opened it for her to enter first. It felt strange to Adrienne, knowing that Janey had actually been here all those years ago. Ahead of her were a flight of stairs, huge she thought, for the hotel as it now was. Obviously, this had once been a grand house, now turned into a fairly second -ate hotel. To her left she saw an elderly lady standing behind a reception desk. Behind her was an array of room keys. Everything looked rather jaded and the thought crossed Adrienne's mind that nothing here had changed for years.

'Bonjour Madame, comment puis-je vous aider?' she asked, and Adrienne hesitated while she searched her schoolgirl French for the translation. *Francois*, meanwhile, stepped forward and asked her to speak English, explaining that Adrienne was visiting from England.

The lady behind the desk immediately apologised and asked the question again, this time in English.

'Ahh! Of course, how can I help you?'

'Ah Madame, thank you. We have a rather strange

request I think,' said Adrienne. 'I am trying to find my mother who went missing from my life in 1962. I have a postcard from her which she sent from Paris at the time, which as you can see, says that she was staying here.'

Adrienne had taken out the postcard and now handed it to the receptionist.

'I also have a photograph of her,' she added, handing over the snapshot of her mother that she had brought with her. 'Do you recognise her?' she continued.

The receptionist looked carefully at both the postcard and the photograph for some moments, before looking up at Adrienne with something of an unexpected expression on her face. In fact, she looked rather cross.

'I am sorry Madame, but this photo doesn't bring back a happy memory for me.'

'Why is that Madame? Please tell me, did something bad happen to my mother when she was here?'

'Well, that I can't say,' the woman replied. 'But I certainly remember her.'

Adrienne's heart thumped in her chest. At last, it seemed she might be getting somewhere. She glanced round at *Francois* saying eagerly 'At last!' But she noticed that for a split second once again his reaction wasn't what she expected. A worried look flashed across his face until he saw her looking at him, when he smiled and said to the receptionist,

'Please Madame, what can you tell us about the

lady in the photo. How long did she stay here and why are your memories of her not happy ones?'

'Monsieur, they are not happy because this young woman left without paying her bill. I never forget people who cheat me and that's why I remember her.

'What! No!' exclaimed Adrienne. 'My mother would never have done a thing like that!'

'Well then,' the woman retorted, 'why did she sneak back in, open her room door without her key by forcing the lock, take all her belongings and leave before any of the staff noticed that she had gone?'

'I just can't believe it!' Adrienne gasped, 'Something must have happened to her.'

'Well, I'm sorry Madame, but that is exactly what happened. Why she did it and where she went to, I have no idea, I'm sorry I can't help you further.'

Adrienne was shocked to the core and utterly confused, disappointed, and fearful as she realised that she had reached a dead end in the quest to find out what had happened to her mum. This had been her only clue and it now proved useless. *Francois* thanked the lady for her help and placed a hand under Adrienne's elbow.

'Come on Adrienne, there's nothing more to be done here,' he said, guiding her to the door.

Once they were out in the street, Adrienne shook his hand away and fought back the tears. She had been so sure that the visit to the hotel would at least provide the next clue in the trail. She had no idea what to do next.

'I'm so sorry Adrienne,' *Francois* said gently. 'It looks as though your mum just wanted to disappear, and if someone wants to do that, there's not much anyone can do to find them.'

Adrienne flashed an angry look at him, saying.

'What! What are you saying? That my mum deliberately walked out on me and came to Paris so that she could just 'disappear', as you put it!? That's utter rubbish. She would never, ever have deliberately left me. Something must have happened to her and I'm not leaving Paris until I find out what.'

'But it's so long ago now,' *Francois* insisted, 'It will be impossible to find out what happened now.'

'Look,' she retorted fiercely, 'that is exactly what I'm going to do. I don't know how yet, but I will. If you want to give up that's fine, I'll do it on my own, but do it, I certainly will!'

Francois looked most uncomfortable, saying 'Please, just think, where on earth will you start? You don't know anyone who knew her here. You don't know where she went when she left the hotel. She could have gone anywhere in the world!'

'You say you knew and loved my mother, when you really have no idea what she was like. I'm telling you she wouldn't have just left me. I can see that you don't believe me, and I think it will be better now if I did this on my own. I want you to leave me alone now please.'

'But Adrienne,' he began, 'I...'

Adrienne turned her back on him and walked away.

She would have to do this on her own. She had no idea how, but she knew she would never give up on her mum. She would find out exactly what had happened to her.

Chapter 15

Prefecture de Police

Armand called after her once and then gave up, realising that he needed to give her some space right now. He also needed space. He needed to think about what had just happened. He felt that the girl was beginning to get far too close to the truth and was determined not to stop until she had uncovered the whole story. Of course, he couldn't let that happen. Whatever she said, he would have to stay close to her at all costs, so that he could intervene in events as and when necessary.

He began to think about how he was going to get her to sign the documents claiming the endowment her father had left her. This, of course, was the main reason he had contrived to be with her in Paris, but he also had to stop her getting at the truth regarding her mother. He would have to get close enough to her for her to trust him and then bring up the subject of the endowment. It would be tricky because she would be wondering 'Why now?' Why hadn't he mentioned it when they were back in England? As for the other matter, he felt reasonably safe. He couldn't see how she could find out about the events of that night ten years ago, but he would be ready with plan B if need be. So, it was important that he found the solution to the endowment trust quickly before events took over and he lost the chance of getting his hands on the money forever. This would all need thinking through carefully.

Meanwhile, Adrienne was walking briskly back towards her hotel. She needed to be alone to consider her next move. After picking up a sandwich and a can of Coke, she asked for her key at reception and made her way up to her room on the second floor. Kicking off her shoes, she flopped onto the bed and let the tears flow, feeling utterly hopeless and bereft of ideas as to what to do next. She had felt so close to getting the answers she needed, and now, she was here, in this strange city whose people with whom she could barely sustain a conversation, and now she didn't even have *Francois* to help her.

She realised if she intended to get to the bottom of this, she couldn't lie here feeling sorry for herself. Getting up, she washed her tear-stained face and freshened up her make up. Although not feeling much like eating, she forced herself to eat the sandwich and drank the coke. Then she began to think about what to do next. She decided to take a walk to clear her head and consider her options. Handing her key in at reception she stepped out into the sunshine and decided on a stroll along the banks of the Seine. Descending the steps onto the promenade, she turned East to admire the architecture of the cathedral from the north side of the river, intending to cross one of the bridges further along in order to take a closer look at the magnificent structure. She knew that architecture had been her mother's passion, and somehow, right now, she felt closer to her as she admired the gothic splendour of Notre Dame.

A little way along Adrienne arrived at the Pont d'Arcole which she judged was the last bridge leading to the Ile de la Cite and the Cathedral. Crossing the bridge, she turned off to the left along the Quai aux Fleurs. It was a pleasant walk along the river. As she approached Pont Saint-Louis bridge, she passed an accordion player giving a rendition of an Edith Piaf song. The music, the Seine, Notre Dame and the smell of Gauloise captivated her senses. Paris was working its magic and she began to feel calmer. She turned right and made her way to the western end of the cathedral, determined to take a look inside.

Not particularly religious, she had nevertheless always enjoyed visiting churches. She found there was always a particular peace in an old church that was rarely found elsewhere. She presumed that all the centuries of earnest worship somehow soak into the fabric of such a place, producing a calm and comforting aura. Notre Dame had accumulated eleven centuries of such an atmosphere and Adrienne felt she needed to wrap it around her now, more than ever. She sat for a while, staring up at the magnificent grandeur of the place, with its beautiful stained-glass windows down either side of the knave and with organ music drifting around her. For the first time since arriving in Paris, she thought about Marge and as she did so, the fog began to clear, and she told herself that she could do this. So, she thought, if I was back in England, where would I start?

Well, she supposed that the first thing she would do would be to talk to the police. If something had happened to Janey, surely the police would have some record; an unsolved crime that may still be on their books? Her stomach churned as the word 'crime' came into her head. Over the years she had sort of come to terms with the thought that her mother might be dead. Now it dawned on her that soon she may have proof of exactly what had happened to her and with that reality would come the grief she had been supressing all these years. Still, knowing the truth was more important than anything else, so visiting the gendarmerie, must be her next move.

Half an hour later she was standing outside the Prefecture de Police on the Ile de La Cite. She had remembered seeing the building on her way back to her hotel. She was very nervous and really had no idea what she was going to say or whether she was even going to be able to make herself understood. Pushing open the heavy glazed door she stepped inside. Ahead of her was a large reception desk and as she walked towards it the young policeman sitting behind it stood up and said,

'Bonjour! Vous desirez, Madame?'

'Oh! Bonjour!' she replied, and then tentatively asked whether he spoke English. She didn't feel her rather poor French was up to the task of explaining what she was looking for.

'Ah, of course, Madame,' he replied, 'how can I help you?'

Adrienne explained that she was looking for information about her mother who had disappeared in Paris in 1962. She added that she was sure that something bad must have happened to her and asked whether they could look through any unsolved crime records that might be relevant. The young officer didn't look hopeful, explaining that all such records were kept in the central records office and it would be impossible to get authorisation to search through them all without having evidence that there had been a crime committed. He went on to say that if her mother had just wanted to disappear there wouldn't be any trace in the police records anyway, particularly as she had never been reported missing.

'But I'm sure she wouldn't have wanted to 'just disappear'!' Adrienne exclaimed. 'What if she'd had an accident, been hit by a car or something. How could I go about finding information about that?'

'Madame, you could try looking through the newspaper records, for any articles relating to an accident or other incident.'

'But how would I do that? As you can see, I don't even speak French!'

'Perhaps I shouldn't say this, but have you thought of hiring a private detective to help you? They would know their way around the records.'

'Well, I hadn't, but since you mention it, maybe I should. I don't suppose you would know of one?'

'Actually, I do, he used to be a policeman but now works as a private detective. I'll write down 'is details for you.'

With that, he wrote a name, address and phone number on a plain record card and handed it to Adrienne, saying,

'There you are Madame. I really hope you will be able to find out what happened to your mother.'

'Thank you so much, you've been very kind' she replied, took the card, and left.

Chapter 16

The Private Detective

Adrienne sat at a table in the window of a little café overlooking Notre Dame. She had just ordered a coffee and croissant and was awaiting the arrival of the *detective prive* Michel Blanc. She had rung him from a call box an hour ago. He seemed keen to meet her to discuss her requirements and arranged to join her at Café Rouge at three o'clock.

She glanced at her watch. It was 2.55pm. She wondered what he would be like. Did he speak fluent English? She certainly hoped so, as she was definitely struggling with his language. A middle-aged man of medium height and build entered the café and looked around, clearly searching for someone. As he saw Adrienne, he caught her eye and gave a slight nod. She didn't know what she had expected but he looked particularly unremarkable, very ordinary in fact. Still, she supposed, that was a good attribute for a detective. It wouldn't do for him to stand out in a crowd.

He made his way over to her table, smiling and stretching out his hand in greeting.

'Mademoiselle Grainger, I presume? Good to meet you.' he said in English with a thick French accent.

'Monsieur Blanc. Thank you for agreeing to see me,' Adrienne replied, shaking his hand and smiling.

He ordered himself a coffee then settled down expectantly in the chair opposite, asking what he could do for her. For some reason Adrienne was particularly nervous and didn't quite know where to start or how much she needed to tell him. She decided that he would need to know as much about her mother as possible, but that more recent events wouldn't be relevant to what she needed him to do.

She told him that she had come to Paris to find out what had happened to her mother who had disappeared apparently without trace, round about 11th March 1962, and she would like his help in trying to find out what had happened to her.

'Ten years is quite a long time,' he replied, and went on to ask her when was she last contacted by her mother.

Adrienne showed him the postcard Janey had sent to Marge, explaining that actually it had only recently come into her possession, which is why she hadn't tried to search before and that until she saw the postcard, she'd had no idea that her mother had even come to Paris, before disappearing.

'I see Mademoiselle,' he said rather pensively. 'Well, there certainly isn't much to go on, is there? I presume you have visited the hotel and also tried approaching the police?'

'Yes, of course,' Adrienne replied, 'There was no clue at the hotel and the police tell me that without actual evidence of a crime having been committed they would be unable to search through the rather extensive records to see what progress, if any, had been made at the time. Of course,' she went on,' there may not have been a crime at all. I'm wondering if she might have had an accident or something.'

'That's possible, of course,' M. Blanc replied. 'If that is the case, there could have been something in the newspapers about it. She was actually in Paris when she disappeared, you say?'

'She was, as far as I know. At least she was when she wrote the postcard.'

'Then a thorough search of the newspapers around that time would seem to be the best place to begin.'

'Is that something you'd be able to do?' Adrienne enquired tentatively.

'Yes, of course. This is something I have often been asked to do. They can be a great source of information. I'm sure I can help you with this initial search. Depending on what we find, further work may be needed.'

'Of course, I understand,' she replied. 'Could I ask what you charge for your services, Monsieur?'

'I charge by the hour Mademoiselle, and for a simple newspaper search that would be 10Fr an hour. Of course, it's difficult to say how many hours work will be required, but I will keep you updated with information about what I have managed to find out.'

'That seems very reasonable Monsieur. How will you contact me?'

'Where are you staying in Paris?' he enquired.

She wrote down the name, address, and telephone number of the Hotel Rivoli on a piece of paper torn from her notebook and handed it to him.

'Now, please tell me all you can about your mother - physical description such as age, height, complexion, hair colour etc.'

Adrienne described her mother to him, which unexpectedly prompted tears to well up in her eyes, partly because she was finding it particularly hard to remember exactly what her mother was like. He could see that she was struggling and asked,

'You wouldn't happen to have a photo as she might have looked at the time?'

'As a matter of fact, yes, I have,' she said with relief and took the photo out of her bag. 'Please take care of it Monsieur, I don't have many photos of her.'

He assured her he would take great care of it and return it to her when his work was done.

'It is rather late in the day now,' he explained, 'so I will start work tomorrow and hopefully should be able to give you some news within the next few days. Of course, you must realise that there may be no news of your mother in the newspapers at all. She may just have wanted to disappear.'

Once more, someone was suggesting that her

mother could have just walked away and left her, and the familiar anger welled up inside her. Her eyes flashed at him and he looked rather taken aback.

'I'm sorry, I didn't mean to upset you, I just wanted to prepare you for every outcome of this search, which may not bring the result you are wishing for,' he explained.

'No, I'm sorry, it's just that people keep telling me that she may have just left of her own accord, but that is something I just can't contemplate.'

'I understand, Mademoiselle. Let us hope then, that we are successful in our work and able to give you some answers.'

With that, he bade her au revoir, said he would leave a message at her hotel as soon as he found out anything useful, and left.

As he walked away, she noticed a woman watching her from one of the tables outside on the pavement. When Adrienne looked at her, she quickly averted her gaze and pointedly looked in the opposite direction. That was all, but it just struck Adrienne as a little odd; no more than that, and she quickly forgot about it. Whilst she was distracted, she hadn't noticed Francois entering the café.

'I didn't expect ....' Adrienne began.

'Oh, sorry,' *Francois* quickly interrupted. 'I just saw you through the window as I was passing. Who was that man I saw you chatting to?'

He turned and beckoned to the waitress, ordering

himself a coffee and a sandwich, and asking Adrienne whether she would like anything else.

Meanwhile, Adrienne, still angry with him and still not completely trusting him, was debating with herself whether to tell him she had engaged Michel Blanc to try to look for information about her mother. In the end, she judged it would be better to have him as an ally than not. Depending what M Blanc discovered, she may still need Francois to help her further down the line.

She explained that he was a private detective and was initially going to search the newspapers from around the time her mother had disappeared, in case she had been involved in an accident or an incident of some kind. *Francois*, she thought, looked a little surprised at the news, but then gathered himself.

'Oh, yes, that seems a sensible place to start if you're determined to carry on with this.'

'Of course I am. Why do you keep inferring that it's pointless to go on with the search?'

'Look,' he began, 'I'm honestly just concerned for you. I just think it would be so much better for you if you could accept it and move on. Now that I have found you, I'll always be here for you, you know.'

Adrienne glanced out of the window and was surprised to see the same woman, still glancing from time to time in their direction. She was around fifty years old, fairly smartly dressed, quite attractive but with a face that told of many struggles in her life. She noticed Adrienne looking at her and this time, she stood up and walked off down the street, quickly disappearing into the crowd.

Distracted by the woman, Adrienne hadn't been concentrating on what *Francois* had said.

'I'm sorry, what did you say,' she asked.

'I said, I'll always be here for you.' he repeated.

Adrienne found this rather embarrassing. She wasn't ready to have him 'always there for her'. She didn't feel she knew him well enough, or trusted him, for that matter. In the end, she said nothing, just nodding slightly in acknowledgement.

Adrienne decided that she needed some space and announced that she was going to go back to her hotel to relax, and that she would let him know when and if she heard anything from M. Blanc. *Francois* gave her details of his hotel and asked her to contact him as soon as she heard anything. He suggested that they meet up the following day so that they could spend some time together, as he had something he wanted to discuss with her that would be important to her future.

'Will you let me buy you lunch? I'll meet you outside the St Michel metro at 12.30, if that's ok for you?'

She gracefully accepted his invitation although not entirely enthusiastic about it.

Chapter 17

The Wait for News

Later that evening, Armand lay on his bed looking up at the ceiling in his hotel room, smoking a cigarette and contemplating his next move. He knew he needed to move fast. Events were moving too quickly for his liking. The girl was obviously determined to find out what had happened to her mother and he had been shocked that she had already engaged a private detective to ferret around. How long would it be before he turned up something? The woman would probably have been pulled from the Seine within days of 'the event' and although not particularly newsworthy, it often being a popular method of committing suicide, the story may well have made the inside pages of one of the newspapers. If the dates tallied, the girl would obviously assume that it might have been her mother. From that point it wouldn't be too difficult for her to gain from the police what information they had. Although he had made sure that there hadn't been anything left in her handbag or the hotel room, to identify her, he couldn't rule out the possibility that they had taken a post-mortem photo of the corpse, which would of course be identifiable from the photo the girl had with her.

Of course, his sole objective, was to get his hands on the money. He'd waited so long for this and he had worked out exactly how he could get her to claim it and how he could simultaneously relieve her of it. He had already primed her regarding his plan. He was to meet her the next day for lunch and intended to tell her about the endowment. He already had the documentation needed for the claim, which now only needed her signature. On the forms he had entered the details for the money to be paid into his own bank account and he would need her to sign the paperwork without looking too closely at it. If she did, he had decided to tell her that the money had to be paid into a French bank account, and that he would transfer it to her once it arrived in his account.

He had felt all along that the girl was sceptical about him. She didn't seem to trust him completely. If he handled this correctly and was convincing enough, he felt sure that she couldn't fail but accept that he was who he said he was. How could she not, when he would be demonstrating that he, 'her father' had always intended for her to receive such a substantial amount of money. Once she had signed the paperwork, given that he knew that here in Paris the Hunters could reappear any time, he hoped to disappear, and he would never need be troubled by her and her wretched mother again. That was plan A. If the detective unearthed anything before he had the signed documentation in his hands, he would have to implement plan B and would have to remain around a little longer, to influence events if need be.

Meanwhile, Adrienne had just finished eating supper in a little café around the corner from her hotel. Her emotions were in turmoil. She knew she was placing huge expectations on M. Blanc and his search of the newspaper archives. She tried to keep herself calm by telling herself that it was a long shot. She also realised that if there was a report which could relate to her mother, the very fact of it being reported in a newspaper would not bode well. It could only be bad news. She had of course, been unconsciously preparing for this day ever since her mother disappeared, but she was only too aware that confirmation of her worst fears would bring to the surface the grief of a twelve-year old girl who's mum never came home. That would be devastating, coming as it did, on top of the grief of losing Marge in such a tragic and sudden way. These thoughts were whirring around in her brain as she stirred her coffee. Then something brought her back to reality with a jolt. She suddenly noticed, sitting at a table across the café, the same woman that had been watching her earlier in the afternoon. Was it just a coincidence, or did this woman have a specific interest in her? She mentally shook herself, telling herself not to be so paranoid, and called the waitress over, asking for her bill.

She walked back to her hotel, deciding on an early night. Tomorrow promised to be a difficult day. She knew she couldn't move far from the hotel as she waited for a message from M. Blanc. She would also be having lunch with *Francois*. He had said that he had something to discuss with her that – how had he put it – would be important for her future. She couldn't imagine what he meant by that, but hoped that he wasn't looking for any long term commitment from her. She wasn't ready for that. There were too many unanswered questions at the moment to think about anything else. As she collected her key from reception she mentioned to the woman behind the desk that she was expecting a message over the next few days from a M. Blanc and she would be grateful if they could let her know immediately if anything did appear. The receptionist made a note and said that if Madame was in the building, she would be notified immediately.

Once in her room, Adrienne kicked off her shoes and decided to take a shower. As she dried her hair in front of the dressing table mirror, she asked herself out loud, 'I hope you're ready for what might come tomorrow,' then immediately replied 'As I'll ever be!' She walked over to the window and took a last look out onto the dark Parisian night, suddenly realising that it was her mother who had brought her to this place at this time, and that despite her having had no connection with her for all these years, her mother was still influencing her life. She mentally swore to her mum that she would find out what had happened to her, whatever, and however long, it took.

Getting into bed, she soon fell into a restless sleep full of images from the previous day, all jumbled up with none of them making any sense. She saw the dark, swirling waters of the Seine, the towering pinnacles of Notre Dame, *Francois* suddenly appearing from nowhere and strangely, that woman who had seemed to be watching them, kept reappearing in her dream.

She woke early, dressed quickly, and couldn't resist ringing reception to see if there were any messages, even though she knew that M. Blanc would hardly have begun his search. Of course, there were none, but she requested that room service bring up some coffee and croissants for her breakfast. After breakfast she decided to take a short walk along the Seine, meaning to return in an hour or so to check the messages. This time, she walked along the promenade to the West, enjoying the sights and sounds of Paris, with the Eiffel Tower in the distance. People were strolling along in the sunshine, mostly in couples and others surrounded by family. Suddenly she felt very alone, allowing herself to think about the future back home in England, without Marge. She hadn't really had time to grieve properly since it happened, after the sudden appearance of *Francois* and then the discovery of the postcard. She knew she would need to give herself time and space when this was all over, to work through it all. Maybe she'd take the Summer break from school to spend a few weeks in Cornwall, a favourite holiday spot she had often visited with her mum and Marge when she was little. Hiring a cottage by the sea she would let the light and the atmosphere work its magic on her.

For now though, she brought her thoughts back to the business in hand. Checking her watch and realised that it was nearly an hour since she'd left the hotel. She retraced her steps and eagerly enquired at reception as to whether there had been any messages. The receptionist informed her that no-one had called or left any notes, so she took her key and went up to her room. She spent the next couple of hours writing in her notebook, an account of all that had happened to her over the last few weeks. She felt it was important to set things down in some kind of order. She supposed it was the schoolteacher in her that demanded the clarity that only a written account of events and feelings could bring. Reading quickly through it afterwards, she realised with some surprise just how sceptical she had become about *Francois*. Before all these events had happened, she would have expected to be thrilled at the prospect of meeting her father. She should have been overjoyed and yet, right from the start, something hadn't sat right with her where he was concerned. All she could do now was to 'sit with it' and see what happened. In the meantime, she decided to try to give him the benefit of the doubt and let his actions speak for themselves.

Checking once more with reception, she found that still nothing had arrived. Due to meet *Francois* at 1pm she decided to get ready and take a leisurely stroll to Café de Flore. She took her time changing into slacks and a cotton shirt blouse, carefully applied her make up and brushed her hair, leaving it to fall freely to her shoulders. Glancing out into the street, the weather didn't look too promising, so she put on her waterproof mac and picking up her umbrella and handbag, left her room and went down to reception. As she approached the desk the receptionist smiled and said,

'Ah! Madame I was just about to call you. A message 'as just arrived for you. Perhaps it is the one you 'ave been waiting for?'

Adrienne eagerly took the envelope and thanked her. Her heart was beating fast as she quickly tore it open. It read:

Mademoiselle Grainger,

I have managed to locate an article which may, and I only say may, relate to your mother. Please meet me at the entrance to the Cite Metro station at 12.15, when I will explain all.

Michel Blanc

Chapter 18

A Body in the Seine

As Adrienne wasn't due to meet *Francois* until one, she was able to see M. Blanc beforehand. Depending on what he had to tell her, she could decide whether to involve *Francois* in the next stage of her quest. It was a short walk to the Cite Metro entrance and as she entered the Place Louis-Lepine, she saw the detective looking around for her as he stood by the railings. As their eyes met, he raised a hand and smiled in recognition.

She quickened her pace, eager to find out what news he had for her. They shook hands and she was thankful that this professional relationship didn't require the customary two kisses.

He gestured to a nearby bench and suggested that they sit down while he explained what he had discovered.

'I have found something in an edition of Le Monde printed about a week after the date on your mother's postcard. I have to warn you that it's not looking good. Are you ready to hear it?'

'Of course, monsieur, I have come this far to find the truth and I have to know, good or bad, what happened to her.'

'Well,' M Blanc went on, 'the article I found relates to the discovery of a body in the Seine.'

He stopped, considerately giving Adrienne time to assimilate the information and process the possible implications. She was looking him in the eye but quickly dropped her gaze to her lap, where her fingers were tightly intertwined as if trying to contain her emotions. After some moments she raised her eyes to his and, her throat constricted with emotion, said quietly,

'Please go on, monsieur.'

'Well, the article didn't give much information, I'm afraid. It simply reported that the body of a woman, aged about thirty, had been recovered from the Seine. The police were investigating the incident, but so far had not been able to ascertain whether it was a suicide, or whether there had been foul play. There was to be a post-mortem examination to determine the exact cause of death.'

As Adrienne listened to all this, she suddenly felt completely detached. She was listening to information about a woman dying in the Seine, but of course, it couldn't possibly have anything to do with her. Most likely it was just a local woman who'd finally succumbed to her demons and in a last desperate attempt to find peace had jumped into the black, welcoming water. She was still completely convinced that her mother would never have done that, leaving her to grow up without her. Her rational brain told her that she couldn't just ignore this news, she would have to investigate it, and asked M. Blanc what he recommended she do next.

'I do think this needs to be followed up with the police,' M Blanc went on. 'If they carried out an investigation, there should be some records on file of that. They may also have in their possession any personal effects found on the body and would quite likely have taken a photograph to be filed, in case someone should come forward to identify the woman in the future.'

He recommended that, armed with this information, she should now return to speak to the police and ask them to search their records for that period, to find out if they had anything that would rule in or out, once and for all, whether this woman was her mother. With that, he handed her a sheet of paper on which he had detailed all the information he had gleaned from the article, saying,

'I will wait to hear from you once you have spoken to the police, and if this person was not your mother, I assume you would want me to go on searching?'

'I would Monsieur. In the meantime, please send me your bill for the work you have done so far. You can leave it at the hotel if that's convenient. I have your card and will call you as soon as I know anything, and in any case, to arrange to pay you.' He handed her mother's photograph back to her, replying,

'Certainly Mademoiselle Grainger.' M Blanc replied, 'I would like to say 'good luck' but given the nature of the news you are searching for, I don't feel it appropriate to do so. Mais, a bientot, Mademoiselle.'

With that, they shook hands and Adrienne was left standing alone in the square staring at the piece of paper he had given her. A nearby clock rang the half hour and dragged her out of her reverie. She was due to meet Francois soon and she wouldn't have time to visit the police station beforehand. She would have to do it later. Should she involve him? Could she trust him to help rather than hinder her, as he had seemed to be doing on more than one occasion during her search. Then she remembered that she had earlier decided to give him the benefit of the doubt. She also felt that she may well need his help with the language, and his local knowledge might be invaluable going forward. So, yes, on balance, she thought, she would put him in the picture when they met.

Armand, meanwhile, had not been idle. He had finalised the paperwork which he had to get the girl to sign, preferably without too much scrutiny, whilst being ready with Plan B if needed. He had then made his way to the Café de Flore on Boulevard St Germain des Pres and booked a table for two. With the document case containing the paperwork under his arm, and feeling rather pleased with himself, he took a leisurely stroll towards the Metro station where he was to meet the girl.

He had been there about five minutes when he spotted her striding towards him. He had to admit, she was a pretty girl, in an understated sort of way. She had a natural grace which he found rather attractive. In fact, he briefly admitted to himself in a rare moment of humanity, that in another life he could have been proud to call her his daughter. However, he quickly dismissed this as sentimental nonsense. He couldn't afford to become fond of her, given what he was about to do to her. As she approached him he could see that she had a purposeful air about her and his heart sank as he realised that she might have had some news from her private detective, which may mean moving to Plan B and delaying his departure. Of course, he put on his usual warm smile in greeting and kissed her on both cheeks, even though he could feel the slight resistance that was always there with her. Adrienne pulled away quickly and as he had already guessed, explained that she'd had some news from M. Blanc, that she needed to discuss with him.

As far as Adrienne was concerned, *Francois*' reaction wasn't quite as she would have expected. In fact, he didn't actually react at all, just saying,

'Of course, well I've booked us a table at the Café de Flore, so we'll be able to have a chat there.'

She would have expected some spontaneous curiosity, but there was none. Once more, she wondered at just how unpredictable he was. He never seemed to react as she imagined he would, somehow. As her natural father she felt there should be more empathy between them.

Chapter 19

The Police Search

As they entered the restaurant a waiter approached and asked if they had a booking.

'Oui,' *Francois* replied, 'Une table pour deux. Le nom est De Havilland.'

Ahh Oui Monsieur,' the waiter nodded, 'Suis moi, s'il vous plait.'

He led them to a table in the far corner of the restaurant. They settled themselves in and *Francois* handed Adrienne the menu, asking what she would like to eat.

'To be honest, I'm not at all hungry,' she blurted, rather sharply. In fact, she was getting quite annoyed with him. How could he not show any interest in what she had learned from M. Blanc? From the minute she'd said she had some news he hadn't even asked her what it was.

'Surely you'll have something?' he pleaded with her.

'Oh, just a piece of quiche and salad please, then.'

'Splendid, I'll have the same.' With that he recalled

the waiter and placed their order, also asking for two glasses of white house wine and a jug of water.

He could see that she was growing impatient to tell him her news and finally asked her what M. Blanc had managed to find out.

To her surprise she felt unable to say the words out loud and instead, handed him the piece of paper M. Blanc had given her. This time, his reaction was entirely predictable, and the colour drained from his face. He looked utterly shocked, which Adrienne interpreted, incorrectly, as grief at the news that his one-time lover and mother of his daughter may have drowned in the Seine, and just around the time he should have been meeting her.

Of course, the truth was rather different. He was certainly shocked, but not grief-stricken. He was shocked that this piece of news now placed Adrienne maybe one step nearer to finding out the truth. Of course, at this point he had no idea what the police would have managed to find out at the post-mortem. The body would certainly have shown signs of a struggle and the cause of death would not have been drowning, because, of course, he knew she had been dead when she hit the water. In which case they may well have concluded that she was murdered. He realised this was a dangerous path he was treading, but he reassured himself, there was absolutely nothing to connect him to the murder, or was there?

'I'm sorry, this must be hard for you too,' she said. 'I

mean, we don't know it was her yet, do we? I still can't believe she would have, you know ....'

'Of course not,' he quickly concurred, 'I can't believe it either.'

'I have to go to the police station this afternoon' she asked him quickly, 'I have to ask them to check the records to find out if there is any evidence that it was her.'

He wondered for a moment whether he ought to go to the police station with her but quickly dismissed the thought. It would be prudent to stay as far away from the police as possible. Of course, he knew that as her father he ought to be supporting her efforts at finding the truth, and said, in as sincere a voice as he could manage,

'This must be so difficult for you Adrienne, and as I've told you before, I'll always be here for you, whatever the outcome.'

This time, when Adrienne heard those words, she was moved by them. Maybe he is genuine, after all, she thought. At that point the waiter returned with their meals which they proceeded to eat in relative silence, each of them engrossed in their own thoughts. One way or another, the afternoon was going to be an ordeal for them both. They concluded their meal with a coffee each, and *Francois* paid the bill.

As they were leaving the restaurant, to her surprise, Adrienne noticed the woman she had seen before, but this time, she was with a man, and they seemed engrossed in an animated conversation and never even looked at her and *Francois* as they walked past. Just coincidence then, she thought.

Francois insisted in walking her over to the police station and half an hour later, they arrived at the door of the Prefecture de Police in the Place Louis-Lepine, opposite Notre Dame cathedral. They had walked, more or less in silence, neither of them wishing to engage in conversation because the topic uppermost in both their minds was prompting thoughts that neither of them wanted to share with the other. Adrienne was trying to push from her mind the thought that the body pulled from the Seine may indeed be her mother. In fact, she certainly couldn't pursue that thought any further, because if it was, neither of the reasons why it may be her, that is suicide or murder, were palatable. Curiously the third possibility – a tragic accident, never even occurred to her.

He hadn't broached the subject of the endowment. He could only bring that up when he was prepared for a quick getaway once the girl had signed the paperwork, but for the moment, he felt the time wasn't right. He needed to find out what the police had discovered about her mother's death first.

Armand briefly considered accompanying her into the building but in the end had decided that it was safer to keep his distance. He was concerned that if he joined her he may have become the focus of attention. Adrienne may have explained who he was and that he had been supposed to meet her mother the night she disappeared. Who knows where that might lead, he thought to himself, I'm better out of it.

'I'll wait for you over there,' he said, pointing to a bench overlooking the square, and then went on, 'Are you sure you want to do this.' he asked her 'are you ready to hear what they may have to tell you?'

'Of course, I'm ready,' she replied sharply, and proceeded to mount the steps in front of the Prefecture.

As she entered, the young officer behind the desk recognised Adrienne and asked, in English, what he could do for her, and had she had any luck with the gentleman he had recommended.

'Yes, thank you, I think we may have some useful information,' she replied, handing him the piece of paper given to her by M. Blanc.

The officer read the paper, then asked her to wait one moment while he went to talk to his superior, to ask what could be done to locate any information that may be held on file. He returned in about five minutes and said,

'Now, it appears that we will need to request a specific search in the Central Records office, which will take a couple of days, but it is more than likely that some record of the post-mortem and any personal effects would have been filed there.'

'Oh, thank you so much,' Adrienne replied, 'that's really helpful.'

'I just need to take a few details from you if you don't mind.'

With that, he proceeded to fill in a form, asking

Adrienne some details about her mother, her physical characteristics, distinguishing marks, and name and address of the subject of the enquiry, stating her relationship to the deceased.' Adrienne found all this very upsetting because it forced her to consider that this body may indeed be her mother, and she was relieved when he reached the end of it.

'As I said, it may take a couple of days,' the young officer told Adrienne, 'so perhaps Madamoiselle could call back on Friday morning when we should have some information for you.'

'Thank you so much,' Adrienne replied, 'I'll see you on Friday, then.'

With that, she stepped out once more into the Place Louis-Lepine, finding that a light shower had blown in on a blustery breeze.

Armand was rather disconcerted when Adrienne told him that it was going to take a couple of days until she had the information she was looking for. He briefly considered trying to get her to deal with the paperwork now, but quickly dismissed that as too risky. He sensed that she still didn't trust him enough to sign anything at his suggestion without full scrutiny of the documents in question. It occurred to him that he could actually make good use of the next two days to pay her some attention, to show her some kindness and gain her trust. Kindness didn't come easily to him, but the stakes were high, and he was determined to get his just rewards for all the years of scheming and plotting that had led him to this point.

Adrienne was now at a bit of a loss as to what to do next. She had to wait at least two days to allow the police time to find the information. She wondered if she could spend some time actually getting to know *Francois* better. There were lots of questions she would like to ask him, about his relationship with her mother and how they came to be separated, but somehow there had never been an appropriate moment, wrapped up as she was in following the trail leading to her mother. Maybe this natural pause in her quest would give her the space to find out more about him.

So it was, that both of them in their own way had reached the same conclusion. The next two days would give them the space to spend time together without the pressure of the search for Janey.

Chapter 20

Two Days in Paris

Over the next two days, *Francois* took her to all of the usual must-see places around Paris. They wandered around Montmartre and climbed the steps to the Sacre Coeur. They strolled through the Bois de Boulogne in the early spring sunshine and lunched in the Café de la Grande Cascade. They climbed the Eiffel Tower as far as it was possible to do so and enjoyed the wonderful views of Paris. Throughout it all he was kind and considerate and Adrienne couldn't help but warm to him.

She began to relax and by the end of the second day spent with him, she felt confident enough in their relationship to ask him about his time spent with her mother. As they sat together, once more at the Café de Flore, after they had finished their meal, she decided to bite the bullet and ask her questions. She wanted to know how they met, how long they had been together, why did they part, and why had she not heard her mother talk about him.

For his part, Armand was grateful that he had carefully read those letters he'd found in the man's apartment, as they had contained most of the information she was asking him for. On the grounds that the most believable lies are the ones that are nearest to the truth, he didn't deviate from the story contained within the letters. Of course, he had to change the end slightly and tell her that there had been a car crash, in which his wife had tragically died. By that time, he told her, he had lost touch with her mother, but of course, he had never forgotten that he had a daughter, and had even made financial provision for her. He told her that once her search was over, he would explain more about that, but it would mean that her future financial security would be assured.

Adrienne couldn't help but be moved when he told her that he had always been thinking about her. For the past two days he had seemed completely genuine and she had to admit that she had begun to believe in him. As he walked her back to her hotel that night, she felt relaxed and allowed herself to feel a glimmer of happiness for the first time since Marge's accident. This time, when he kissed her on both cheeks to say goodnight, she didn't resist.

It wasn't lost on Armand that she hadn't pulled away quickly as he kissed her goodnight. Job done, he thought. It had been a bit of a struggle for him, but he seemed to have won her over. He'd also managed to plant a seed regarding the money, which he could capitalise on when the time was right. He decided to walk back to his hotel. He needed to think about what might occur tomorrow and how he was going to handle it, depending on what the police told the girl. If the conclusion they had come to was that it was murder, he would need to act quickly as he couldn't risk them finding out that he had been supposed to meet the woman which might result in them opening the case again. On the other hand, if they had concluded it was suicide or an accident, he could take things a little slower, show the girl some compassion and then conclude his plan before disappearing. Either way, he could be out of Paris within a few days and this whole episode in his life would be over. He had made the decision not to return to Singapore. He would go instead to South America. He had heard that the 'Hunters' rarely ventured there.

In her hotel room, Adrienne's feelings were confused. She had to admit, she had spent a pleasant couple of pleasant days with *Francois* and he had gone out of his way to make her feel special. A lot of the questions surrounding his relationship with her mother had been answered and she was thrilled to hear him say that he had never forgotten about her. Of course, these pleasant thoughts were clouded by what was going to happen in the morning. What was she going to find out? That her mother had been murdered or that she had jumped of her own free will into the Seine, leaving her behind?

She slept pretty well, considering her confused state of mind, and woke quite early. She had arranged to meet *Francois* near the entrance to the Cite Metro at 9.30. She was showered and dressed by 8.30 and just had time to grab a coffee and croissant at the Café Rouge before making her way to the Place Louis-Lepine. She was actually looking forward to seeing him again. She knew the day may be a difficult one for her and she was glad she would have his support.

When they met, with a rather uncustomary show of empathy, he asked her how she was feeling about what was to come.

'I'm ok,' she replied. 'To be honest it will be a relief, whatever the news.'

In truth she was, of course, rather anxious, not just at what she might hear from the police, but at how she would deal with that knowledge. If the body they'd found was that of her mother, it would once and for all end any dreams she may have harboured that she would one day find her again. It would be confirmation that she would be alone for the rest of her life. She would belong to no-one.

Chapter 21

News From the Archives

They arrived at the police station and *Francois* hesitated. He would have liked to be present at her interview with the police, but in the end once again decided it was just too risky. He knew that if he was there, he may be confronted with the evidence of the incident which he had hoped he could have left conveniently filed to the back of his mind. He would have to be on his guard. After all, the police were trained to spot any giveaway signs. He just couldn't take the risk and said he would wait outside for her.

Adrienne had to admit that she was rather disappointed. She had hoped that after the couple of days they had spent together he would have understood she might need his support, given the news she could be about to receive. Of course, she was getting used to his unpredictability, and hesitated for only a second before taking a deep breath and mounting the steps alone.

Adrienne approached the desk and the young officer looked up and smiled at her. This was a different one than the young man she had seen a couple of days ago.

'Bonjour, Madame,' he said, 'Comment puis-je vous aider?'

'I'm sorry Monsieur, my French....'

'Ah, no problem Madame. 'How can I help you?'

Adrienne explained who she was and that she had requested information about an incident which had happened some time ago and had been told to call back in a couple of days to see if anything had been found.

'One moment,' he replied, 'I will check if we have news for you.'

He disappeared through the door at the back of the room. Adrienne was feeling nervous now. Was she finally going to find out what had happened to her mother, after all these years?

The officer returned quickly, saying that they did in fact have some news for her, but would she please follow him to somewhere more private, when it would all be explained to her. She followed the officer into the Interview Room. Adrienne focussed her full attention on the man behind the desk. He gestured to her to take the seat opposite, saying,

'Good morning Madam, please sit down. I'm Inspector Farrand.' He extended his hand in greeting.

'Good morning, Monsieur,' she responded,

The Inspector spoke to Adrienne,

'First of all, if you don't mind, I will need to check your identity. Do you have your passport with you?'

'Of course,' Adrienne replied, taking it out of her handbag and handing it to the Inspector.

She noticed he had a large brown envelope in front of him on the desk and her heart skipped a beat as she saw that it had the words 'NUMERO DE DOSSIER 15362' typed on a label fixed to the front. With her pulse racing she realised this must contain what she was looking for.

After checking her passport and returning it to her, he turned his attention to the envelope, placing a hand on it and saying,

'Well, Madam, we have managed to locate the file relating to the incident reported in Le Monde about which you were enquiring. I believe that you think the person involved could be your mother, is that correct?'

'Well, yes,' Adrienne replied quickly, 'I mean, it looks as though this happened just about the time that she was in Paris and just disappeared without telling us where she was going. I haven't heard from her since.'

'I wonder, Mademoiselle, do you have a photograph of your mother?'

'Yes, I do,' she replied, taking the photo from her handbag and passing it to him, 'it was taken just before she disappeared.'

The Inspector looked at the photograph and she

could see from his reaction that he already suspected what she was about to face. Her stomach lurched.

'I expect that, after all this time, you are eager to know, one way or the other whether this was her. In that case, if you are ready, we will take a look. I have to warn you that there weren't many clues as to the identity of the woman, but there is a photograph, taken post-mortem. I don't need to tell you that if it is your mother you may find it upsetting to look at.'

Adrienne, who was trembling with apprehension, could do no more than nod in agreement.

With that, the Inspector opened the envelope and retrieved the contents. Adrienne could see that there was a typed up written report, presumably some kind of incident report. There was other paperwork, maybe the post-mortem details, and also what Adrienne could tell was the reverse of a photograph.

'Are you prepared, Madame.' he asked gently.

Adrienne nodded and he turned the photograph over. As she looked at it, her body seemed to flow downwards towards her feet. She felt faint and if she hadn't been sitting would probably have slid to the floor. She knew instantly that the face, that dead face, which was white, whose lips were blue, was her mother. And yet, it wasn't her mother. It could never be her mother. She was warm and bright and alive, not this dead thing she was looking at. She looked away, unable to bear the sight any longer. She was feeling numb now. So that's it, she thought, it's over. Mum's gone for ever. No more hoping. She fought to control her emotions.

'There were no personal effects on the body, except this,' the Inspector told her, removing something from a paper envelope. It was a gold chain with a locket attached. Adrienne caught her breath as she looked at it. The memory of it hanging around her mother's neck flooded back into her mind and she couldn't stop the tears any longer. She fumbled in her handbag for her handkerchief.

The Inspector opened the locket and inside was a small photo of a child. Obviously, it had suffered some deterioration, but he could still see that it was indeed a younger version of the young lady sitting in front of him. This, combined with the similarity between the postmortem photograph and the one she had handed to him earlier, convinced the Inspector that this was indeed the young lady's mother.

'Can I get you a drink of water, or a coffee Mademoiselle?' he asked.

'Thank you, a coffee, please,' she replied, glad of a moment or two to gather herself.

He lifted the phone on the desk and asked whoever had picked up, to bring a coffee for Mademoiselle Grainger.

'When you are ready, perhaps we can discuss what our investigations revealed at the time?' he suggested.

Taking a deep breath, Adrienne said 'Of course, carry on. Please Monsieur.'

Taking up the written report the Inspector quickly

scanned through it. He then explained to Adrienne that her mother's body had been taken from the Seine on the morning of 13th March 1962. A postmortem had been carried out and the cause of death found to be drowning.'

The Inspector had paused to let Adrienne take the information in, then went on,

'There had been however, an unexplained blow to the head, which seemed to have occurred shortly before death. This could, the report says, have occurred whilst she was in the water, perhaps from her head striking a bridge upright as she was thrown around in the current. The inquiry concluded that the cause of death was probably either accidental, or by suicide, but because neither could be proved conclusively, the official verdict stated that the cause of death was 'undetermined'.

Adrienne's mind grasped at the word 'accidental'. At last, here was something that she could grab hold of. Some explanation that didn't involve abandonment. She had never believed that her mother would have left her by choice. But an accident! That was something she may be able to accept. Accidents happen, she knew that only too well, after Marge!

A police officer appeared and placed the coffee on the desk in front of Adrienne, then the Inspector continued,

'I know this is difficult for you Mademoiselle, but we will need to complete some official paperwork so that a death certificate can be issued for your mother now that, as her next of kin, you have been able to identify her.'

'I understand Monsieur,' Adrienne replied softly.

'Before we do,' the Inspector continued, 'do you have any further questions?'

Adrienne thought for some moments before asking 'Could you tell me where she was found?'

'According to the report she was pulled from the water near the Pont d'Lena, at the Port Debilly, just opposite the Tour Eiffel. Someone reported seeing a body in the water and the Brigade Fluvial retrieved it almost immediately.'

'And where did they think she had fallen into the water?'

'Well, Mademoiselle, that is a little difficult to say but the report does suggest that she probably entered the water somewhere around the Ile de la Cite.'

Adrienne shivered. She remembered the feeling she'd had standing looking down at the water near the Square du Vert-Gallant on that first day, and now she was sure that must be the spot.

'What happened to my mother's body, Monsieur?'

'It would have been held until after the inquiry was complete and then the judge would have released it for burial or cremation. As there was no clue as to her identity, which meant that no relatives could be contacted to arrange burial, the body would have been cremated.'

'And the ashes?' Adrienne went on, hoping that she

could at least take her mother's ashes home to be buried with her grandmother and Marge.

'I'm sorry Mademoiselle, this must be very hard for you. They would have been kept for twelve months after cremation and if unclaimed in that time, would have been scattered in the Garden of Remembrance in the Pere Lachaise Cemetery, here in Paris.'

Adrienne's shoulders visibly sank as she heard this news. She wouldn't even be able to give her mother a decent funeral. The tears welled up in her eyes once more.

'If you have no more questions, Mademoiselle, could we please complete the official documentation? Once this is done, it will be submitted to the Court and the acte de deces, the death certificate, as you would say, will be forwarded to you in due course.'

Once the documentation was completed, Adrienne got up to leave and thanked the Inspector for his help. He asked her if she would like to take the locket with her and she readily accepted.

As she left the prefecture, she could see *Francois* sitting on the bench across the square. Right now, she would have preferred to be alone, but he also had a right to know what she had just been told, and so she walked over to him.

As she approached *Francois*, he could see that she was upset, which he supposed was to be expected. He stood up as she approached and said,

'Adrienne, what did they say?'

'Well, it was all difficult to hear, but there is no

doubt that the body pulled from the water was mum. He had a post-mortem photograph, and the locket that she always wore. It's all so final now, that's what's so hard.'

At that, the tears welled up in her eyes once more and she had to take a moment or two to steady her emotions. They both sat down on the bench and then Adrienne went on,

'The police told me that the post-mortem had indicated that she had drowned, and the inquest decided that the cause was 'undetermined', but likely to be accidental.'

Armand's ears pricked up at this news. So, she had still been alive when she went into the water! In his most sincere voice he said,

'Adrienne, I'm so sorry you had to hear that, but perhaps you'll be able to move on, now that you know what happened to her.'

This man is so unbelievably crass she thought to herself. As if she would ever 'move on' as he put it; he has no idea how I feel! She said nothing, what was the point, he would never understand her.

'What will you do now,' he asked.

'Well, there's nothing for me here now,' she replied, 'There isn't even a grave for me to visit. I feel that I just want to go home.'

Saying that he would be sorry to see her leave and realising that time was running out for him to get her to sign the paperwork, he invited her to join him for supper that evening. They arranged to meet at seven thirty in the Place Dauphine, as he said there was a good restaurant there, where they could get some dinner.

Chapter 22

Lauren

Ten minutes later Adrienne lay on the bed in her hotel room, clutching her mother's locket and going over the morning's events in her mind. She now knew the facts of her mother's disappearance, or most of them. She knew that Janey had fallen into the Seine and drowned, but it was as though this was all about someone else's life. The plot of a third-rate novel. She seemed unable to assimilate these facts into her own story. She tried to imagine these events occurring while she, age twelve, was sitting in the classroom listening to her teacher, or maybe she had been eating supper with Aunt Marge as her mother was fighting for her life in the murky waters of the Seine! And during all those years afterwards, when she had been trying to imagine what had happened to her mother, in fact, her mother was already gone, cremated, and her ashes scattered in a Parisian cemetery. It just seemed incredible, and yet, she had just seen the proof with her own eyes.

She was now certain in her own mind that her

mother's death was an accident, she had not deliberately committed suicide, leaving her behind. This was something she knew she could eventually come to terms with. She now knew that she wasn't in any way to blame for Janey's death. Although her adult brain had long been telling her that it couldn't be her fault, her twelve year old brain had still, from time to time, told her that she must have done something wrong for her mother to leave her without a word. Maybe now she could stop feeling guilty of being in some way responsible for her disappearance.

Of course, she realised, she still had no idea why her mother had come to Paris, or who she had been supposed to meet. What was so important that she could leave home without a word of explanation? Yes, she knew how Janey had died but there was still much that she didn't know. Why was she even in Paris in the first place? She decided that was one mystery that may never be solved. Would she ever know what events had actually led to her losing her mother?

For the first time in all those years, she was feeling angry, not at her mother, but at the way life can be so cruel. How could some split-second decision her mother had taken, or a particular path she had chosen to walk, at a certain day and time, have resulted in her death and changed her own life forever? And of course, how could Marge, being distracted by seeing her walking down the street, precisely in the same moment as some mad-cap idiot had driven his car round the corner, have caused her death too? Life's a bitch, she thought, thumping the pillow in anger and regret as tears began to flow.

Gradually, she calmed down, and was left feeling utterly spent and somehow empty, numb of all feeling. She dragged herself off the bed, washed her face, reapplied her make up and brushed her hair, before carefully placing the locket in the side pocket of her holdall. Even though she didn't feel particularly hungry, she decided to go over to the Café Rouge.

The café was fairly empty. Just a few tourists sitting around drinking coffee and chatting. She sat down towards the back of the room, feeling that all she wanted was to blend into the background and think. As the waiter approached, she ordered a sandwich and café au lait. After about five minutes she noticed the middle-aged woman that she had seen several times over the last few days, enter the café. The woman was looking at her and made straight for her table.

Smiling at Adrienne, she put out a hand in greeting and said

'Bonjour Mademoiselle. May I join you?'

Adrienne was rather taken aback. By the way the woman had addressed her, it was obvious that she knew she was English.

'Bonjour Madame,' Adrienne responded, 'I'm sorry, I have seen you around a few times, but have we actually met before?'

'No Mademoiselle, we haven't. I'm Lauren,' she replied, 'May I sit down?'

'Err yes, of course, although I'm afraid I won't be good company today. I've got rather a lot on my mind.'

The woman sat down opposite Adrienne and looking genuinely concerned, said,

'Yes, I know, and I'm so sorry for your loss. It must have been a hard thing to hear.'

Adrienne was genuinely shocked that this rather mysterious woman appeared to know about the day's events and quickly asked her how on earth she did know.

'I am sorry Mademoiselle, we need your help, but before approaching you, we had to know why you are here in Paris. We have many sources, and it wasn't too difficult to discover your sad story.'

Adrienne was rather annoyed at this intrusion into her life, but she was also intrigued.

'I see,' Adrienne retorted, 'Well in that case, I think you owe me an explanation Madame.'

'Of course,' Lauren replied. 'I will tell you everything. The story is a long one Mademoiselle, but it is one that you need to hear. In the end your own life may depend on it.'

Adrienne stared at her in disbelief. Could this day bring yet more revelations? Could she bear it?

'Is it about my mother and what happened to her? The Inspector told me it was probably an accident.'

'That may well be true,' Lauren went on, 'but the story is only indirectly connected to your mother, it is actually about your father and what happened to him.'

'Happened? What do you mean 'happened', he's here in Paris, right now.' Adrienne quickly blurted out.

'No Adrienne, may I call you that?' Lauren asked quietly. 'He isn't, but that is only part of it. I need to tell you the whole story if you are willing to listen. But we need to go somewhere more private. Can we do that?'

Adrienne had, of course, always had her suspicions about *Francois* although in the last few days had begun to trust him. Now this woman, this perfect stranger, was implying that in fact he wasn't her father after all. Of course, she needed to hear what the woman had to say, but could she trust her any more than she could trust *Francois*, and asked her outright, why she should do that.

Lauren looked her straight in the eye, and something about her directness moved Adrienne.

'Because, Adrienne, I have lived the story I am about to tell you for many years. It has shaped my life since I was younger than you are today. The man who calls himself your father has been in this story from the very beginning and now I have to bring it to an end, but I need your help. Will you at least listen to what I have to say? I beg you.'

Lauren seemed so genuine and what she was saying was so shocking that Adrienne knew she couldn't refuse her.

'I'm staying at the hotel across the road,' she said, 'maybe we could go up to my room, we won't be disturbed there.'

The woman looked relieved and answered, 'That would be perfect Adrienne, thank you.'

Chapter 23

Lauren's Story

Adrienne sat opposite Lauren in the hotel room, nervously waiting for her to begin. She was feeling pretty bruised. The events of this day were already ones she would never forget, and now she was about to hear news she felt was just as momentous as the information she had already been given by the police.

Lauren began,

'Thank you for agreeing to listen to what I have to say. You may find some of it hard to believe, but I promise you that every word is true.'

'Please, go on,' Adrienne answered quickly, not wishing to prolong matters.

'The story really begins in 1942, when the man you know as Francois De Havilland was a policeman serving in the Paris police force. His name then was Armand Bouchard. I don't know whether you've heard of Le Raffle, Mademoiselle, but this was a brutal operation to round up Jews in order to imprison them and in most cases, to eventually annihilate them. It was carried out on the orders of the Nazis but the fact is that it was the French police who actually did their dirty work. This is denied by the authorities of course, but we, who were there, we know who did this. On one occasion, Jews were being taken from their homes at a moment's notice, marched through the streets, loaded onto buses and taken to internment camps. They were kept there for days with little water or food. We are talking of many thousands of men, women and children. From there they were taken as forced labour or sent to extermination camps where most were gassed and their bodies incinerated.'

Lauren paused here, to allow time for Adrienne to comprehend the enormity of what she was telling her.

'I had no idea ....' Adrienne whispered, 'Of course, I had heard about the concentration camps but the way you put it – it sounds so matter of fact.'

'And that is the way it was done. As though this was the most natural thing in the world; to take men, women and children and exterminate them, just because they were Jews. I said that French policemen were the ones who carried out the rounding up and internment of these people, and one of these policemen was Armand Bouchard. This was a man I knew. He came from our neighbourhood before the war. You can imagine the terror of being dragged out of your home with no time to gather any belongings. If anyone resisted, the police shot them without hesitation, presumably to deter others from attempting it.

'You may wonder how I know all this Mademoiselle. I know it because I was there. I was there with my mother and my brother and sister. They came into our neighbourhood one day and forced us at gunpoint into the street. A young man who had been standing near us, tried to run away. Armand Bouchard opened fire and the young man fell, along with two other people who had been sprayed indiscriminately with bullets, including my mother. Can you believe it Mademoiselle, they left the dead where they fell. I tried to hold on to my mother, but Bouchard knocked me away with the butt of his rifle and I was dragged away by my brother. At twelve years old I had to leave my mother lying in the dust and filth of the street of the ghetto. Even at that young age I swore that one day, Bouchard would pay.

The next time I saw him was when they were loading us onto the trains to take us to the east. I was with my brother and sister. Bouchard was there, in charge of forcing the people into the filthy trucks. I saw him only briefly before they slammed the doors shut on us.

We were first of all taken to a Labour Camp where we were forced to work fourteen hours a day with little food and in terrible living conditions. Anyone who became unfit for work disappeared, probably shipped off to one of the extermination camps, although at the time, we did not know where they had gone. Some died there of course, through exhaustion and starvation. I was strong and also determined to survive. I was not going to let my mother's death go unpunished. My every waking hour was filled with thoughts of revenge.

I knew I must remain alive and, one day, gain justice or retribution for my mother. Eventually as the war was nearing its end, the Nazis, in an attempt to cover up what they had done to us, marched us many miles to an extermination camp. We were so weak that many collapsed on the way and were shot where they lay. Again, I managed to stay alive, my mother's face always before me; my brother and sister did not. Thank God, I was still alive, although barely, when the Allies arrived.

Lauren paused again, struggling to contain her emotions. Adrienne could see how hard this was for her.

'I'm so sorry Madame,' she whispered.

After a few moments, Lauren continued,

'After liberation, we who had survived, slowly recovered our strength and sanity, and as we did so, we began to band together to attempt to bring to justice those who had inflicted such horrors on our people. In 1952, I joined with a group of people intent on hunting down as many of the Nazis or their collaborators as we could find. Over the years we have had many successes, but many have still escaped justice. One of these is Armand Bouchard, who of course, had always been at the top of my list.

'In 1954 we almost had him. We knew he was working in the Paris Mortuary and had been watching him for several days. Then one day, he wasn't there anymore. He must have noticed that he was being watched and had disappeared. We later found out that he must have exchanged identities with a body that had been brought into the mortuary. He had covered his tracks well and we were unable to find out the name of the man with whom he had exchanged identities.

'It was many years later that we picked up his trail once again. He was spotted in Marseilles, working in a bar, under the name Francois De Havilland, leading us to believe that this was the name of the man whose body had turned up in the mortuary. From his subsequent actions I think we can now conclude Mademoiselle, that this man was indeed your father.'

Adrienne was shocked. This was beginning to make some sense.

'Only last night, Madame, he told me about a motor accident in which his wife was killed!' she said, 'Did he evade you again?'

'He did. Just as we were about to take him, he disappeared again and until he turned up here last week, we had no idea where he was.'

Adrienne asked 'When did he disappear from Marseilles?'

'That was in March of 1962.' Lauren replied.

'That was when my mother came to Paris. 11th March 1962! He told me that my mother had asked to meet him but never turned up. We now know that my mother actually died the next day, apparently accidentally falling into the Seine.'

'Adrienne, I fear that accidental deaths do not occur around M. Bouchard.'

Chapter 24

The Plan

Adrienne's emotions were in turmoil at the implication that *Francois* may have been involved in Janey's death.

'But why would he have wanted to kill my mother? But of course,' she went on, 'she would have known he was an imposter. Then again, Mum said that she was going to meet someone who would give her the answers she needed, which sounded like he had invited her to come to Paris to give her some information. But about what exactly? Unless – what if he'd asked her to meet him, but not using Francois' name, maybe even his own name? But why did he need her to come to Paris? In any case he insisted to me that he never saw her in Paris in March 1962, and that he left for Singapore the next day where he remained until he saw news of my Aunt's death and came to find me.'

Lauren didn't interrupt. She could see that Adrienne needed to work all this out for herself.

After a moment or two Adrienne continued, 'But,

if as you say, he is not my father, I don't understand why he would leave Singapore where he hadn't been detected, to come to England to find me, putting himself in danger of detection once again. Unless it's something to do with this trust fund he has told me he set up for me after he visited my mother for the last time. But of course, it would have been my real father who did that. Perhaps it was set up so that only I can claim it. Maybe that's why he needs me, to claim the money and then he intends to take it from me somehow.'

'I fear there are still many mysteries to solve here Adrienne, and the only person who has the answers is Armand Bouchard. But if you are right and he needed you to claim the money, you are in more danger than I imagined. Once he has the money, I'm sure he intends to leave the country immediately, and he won't leave you behind as a witness to what he has done. You are a 'loose end' that he will not hesitate to eliminate.'

Adrienne shivered. If this man is as ruthless as I'm being told, he may well have been responsible for Mum's death, she thought. Maybe it wasn't an accident after all!

'Will you help me Adrienne?' Lauren asked, 'It won't be without its dangers of course, but we will be there to protect you, you have my word.'

Adrienne knew she had to help this woman. This man had not only caused the deaths of many innocent people either directly or by handing them over to the Nazis, he had stolen her father's identity, but may also have been responsible for her mother drowning in the Seine. He mustn't be allowed to get away with it.

'What do you intend to do with him?' she asked Lauren.

'We intend to take him and bring him to justice for all the war crimes he committed while working for the Nazis, and, if he did have a hand in your mother's death, for that too. We do have some evidence against him but in order to ensure conviction after all this time, we do need to hear him admit to his crimes.'

'And what would you want me to do?' Adrienne went on.

'Where have you arranged to meet him?'

'In the Place Dauphine at seven thirty, when we're meant to go out for dinner somewhere around there. I want to throw some flowers in the Seine for Mum beforehand though.'

'Then, maybe you could meet him as arranged and suggest that you first go to throw the flowers in the river. Where do you intend to do that?'

Adrienne told her she knew exactly where she must do it, and that was, as it happened, quite close by, in the Square du Vert-Gallant, on the Ile de la Cite, because that is where she believed her mother had fallen into the water.

'Mais, that is perfect,' Lauren continued. 'All you have to do is to lead him down the steps and into the park to its westernmost point and throw your flowers into the water for your mother. It will be quiet there at that time, and quite dark by then. Then, and this, of course, will be the dangerous moment, confront him with his real identity as a Nazi collaborator and demand he tells you what really happened to your mother. My guess is that he will not be able to resist bragging about how he fooled you both. We will be there, out of sight, listening to his confession. If he attacks you, we will be there to save you.'

Adrienne immediately realised that she would be putting herself in considerable danger, but she also knew that it had to be done. How else would she ever get at the whole truth about her mum, and if he was responsible, she owed it to her to get some justice for the years he had taken from her.

'Very well, madame, I will help you.' she said. She realised that she was placing a lot of trust in this woman who she had only just met, and yet, if felt right. It felt as if a piece of a jigsaw had fallen into place. She supposed that was because of all the little incidents that had caused her to suspect *Francois* or Armand, or whatever he called himself. Her instincts had been right all along then.

The two of them finalised the arrangement and Lauren left, leaving Adrienne to her own thoughts. She was, of course, very anxious and not a little afraid. What if Lauren and her friends let her down. What if everything she had told her was wrong and *Francois* was genuine after all. As soon as that thought arose, she dismissed it. She had doubted him from the start, and on the other hand Lauren seemed genuine. She had to go through with this. As Lauren had said, there were still too many mysteries to be solved, and only he had the answers.

Remembering that she needed to pick up some flowers for her mother, she threw on her coat and left the hotel, striding purposefully towards the Pont Notre Dame. In five minutes, she was in the Marche aux Fleurs. She chose a bunch of white flowers for her mother then hurried back to the hotel, needing some time to unwind before getting ready for her meeting at seven thirty.

By seven-fifteen she was making her way along the Seine towards Pont Neuf feeling very nervous. This was a huge thing she was about to do, and she knew it only too well. Crossing the bridge, she turned left into the narrow entrance of the Place Dauphine. She saw him immediately, standing in the middle of the Place, looking around, obviously searching for her. Her stomach lurched at the sight of him and she felt decidedly nauseous. After all that she had heard earlier, just the sight of him disgusted her. However, she took a deep breath and strode towards him.

Chapter 25

The Finale

Armand had been feeling quite satisfied with the events as they had unfolded and had enjoyed a hearty lunch in the hotel restaurant. He had felt that at last things were going his way. He would take the girl out for dinner that evening and get the documents for release of the trust fund monies signed, and by this time tomorrow would be on his way to a new life.

He had spent the afternoon preparing for his departure. He checked the times of the flights from Paris to Argentina. He would need to be at the airport by 10am in the morning. He packed his bags and carefully placed his 'Francois De Havilland' passport along with the documentation the girl would later sign, in his document case.

He decided to take a long hot bath, then shaved and dressed, ready for the last meeting with his 'daughter'. He would be so relieved not to have to continue this charade. He was growing weary of it and was eager to leave it all behind and to turn to the future, far away from Paris and the Hunters.

He had begun to feel pretty secure as far as they were concerned. He hadn't had sight of them since he left Marseilles in 1962, but of course, he knew they were still around and had no doubt that given half a chance they would take him. He also knew that they were active across the world, they never gave up, but he was aware that Argentinian authorities were actually quite protective of people like him, who had worked for the Fuhrer. He felt that he would be relatively safe there, particularly with his French passport.

He made his way to the Place Dauphine, arriving at seven-twenty-five. He would buy her dinner first, he thought, and then explain about the documents that needed her signature. Once she had signed them, he would make some excuse about not feeling well or something – he hadn't decided exactly what, make his exit, and that would be that. He would never have to see her again.

Still, he wasn't quite there yet, and as he saw her approaching, he smiled broadly and held out his arms to greet her. He kissed her on both cheeks and once again noticed her reluctance. Stupid woman, he thought. What's the matter with her now? Still, what does that matter, after tonight I won't have to bother with her again. He noticed she was carrying a bunch of flowers which he thought was rather odd, musing wryly, surely they weren't for him.

For her part, Adrienne had forced herself to smile

at him and even allowed him to kiss her in greeting. She couldn't risk alarming him, she thought.

'There is a nice little restaurant around the corner,' he said. 'Shall we go?'

'Before we do,' Adrienne replied, a little nervously, he thought, 'I would like to throw these flowers in the water, for my mother.'

He was a little taken aback, wondering why anyone would bother to do such a thing, but decided to humour her, replying,

'Yes, of course, where would you like to do it.'

'From the Square du Vert-Gallant I think, which as you know, is just over the road.'

This suggestion rang some alarm bells in his head, and he immediately wondered why she had chosen the very spot where the woman had met her end, and he quickly asked her,

'Why there?'

'Because the Inspector said that my mother probably fell into the water from the Ile de la Cite and that is the westernmost point of the island, so it just seemed to make sense to do it there,' she explained.

It did seem a plausible explanation, and after all, he did enjoy the irony of these little coincidences.

They made their way out of the Place and across the Place de Pont Neuf to the stairs leading down into the park. Adrienne could feel her legs trembling as she descended the steps which were dark and narrow. It was dusk now and she was beginning to regret ever agreeing to do this. As they emerged from the stairs, she could see that there was hardly anyone in the park, just one or two people at the near end.

Armand could sense that the girl was nervous. Maybe it was because she was thinking of her mother. After all it was only this morning that it had been confirmed to her that she was actually dead, and now no doubt, she would be reflecting on what she was about to do.

They entered the park and Adrienne led the way, making for the narrow, pointed end of the promontory. She glanced around nervously but there was no one else at all at this end of the park, as far as she could see. Either they were well hidden, or she was on her own, she thought. Her knees were literally knocking as she reached the end, beneath a weeping willow tree. She was relieved to see that there were bushes to either side where she was praying that Lauren and her friends would be hiding. She fervently hoped they were. It was too late to back out now.

Well, this is fun, he thought, may as well humour her as it seems important to her. I've got to keep her on side, until I get that signature. The girl was now standing at the very end of the park with her head bowed, obviously 'communing with her mother I suppose' he thought scornfully. He couldn't believe she had managed to choose the very spot where the woman had slid into the water all those years ago. That delicious irony again! He watched as she threw the flowers onto the water one by one.

When she had finished, Adrienne stood for some

moments summoning up the courage for what she was about to do. She looked up, and in the distance, she saw the Eiffel Tower against the night sky. I wonder whether that was the last thing mum saw, she thought. With that, she took a deep breath, turned to him, paused and said,

'I know who you are,'

He was shocked, not only at the words she had spoken, but at their vehemency.

'What do you mean,' he retorted, 'I'm your father!'

'No, you're not,' she replied with as much conviction as she could manage, 'You are Armand Bouchard and you stole my father's identity.'

He moved towards her and she took a step back but then stood her ground, while saying,

'I want to know what happened to my mother, what did you do to her?'

Where is she getting all this from, he wondered angrily.

'What are you talking about? I know nothing of this Armand Bouchard, or what happened to your mother.' he insisted.

'But you see, I know all about you. You were a Nazi collaborator in the war, and responsible for many deaths.'

At that moment he realised the game was up. The Hunters must have got to her, which meant they knew he was here in Paris. Those bastards are determined to get me, he thought. Well, I've escaped their clutches more than once and I will do again. As for this stupid girl, what a complete waste of his time it's been, and it was because he'd left Singapore to find her, that had given the Hunters the chance to find him again.

'You, you are just as stupid as your mother. She came to Paris just because I a perfect stranger, asked her to. Oh, I did meet her, and it was right here on this spot, can you believe? And now, here you are, and it looks as though history is about to repeat itself. Would you like to join her?'

Adrienne was moving backwards but couldn't move any further because she was up against the railings. Somehow, she summoned up the courage to say,

'You won't get away with it, people are here who know all about what you did, you were a traitor to your country and an evil murderer of innocent people.'

'Innocent people?' he sneered, 'They weren't people, they were vermin and they had to be put down. The Fuhrer showed us how to deal with them and I was proud to do it. Yes, they deserved to be put down, just like you!' he exclaimed as the anger welled up in his chest and he couldn't help himself, he struck Adrienne with huge force across her face and she fell down. She was dazed but still conscious as she watched two men emerge from the shadows.

They tried to grab him by the arms to restrain him, but he shook them off. One of them then hit him with his fist in his face, while the other one struck him with something that looked like the butt of a gun across the back of his head. He dropped like a stone, striking his head on a nearby boulder. As she watched, the men bent down to look at him more closely and one of them felt for a pulse.

They exchanged some muffled phrases that Adrienne couldn't make out and seemed to be deciding what to do. Then to her surprise, after looking around to make sure there was no one about, they lifted his lifeless body over the railings and then pushed it over the edge of the parapet into the black, swirling waters of the Seine.

After picking up the document case he had dropped, without a word they disappeared into the darkness as quickly as they had come.

Adrienne got up slowly, a little light-headed, but able to walk. She was trembling and deeply shocked at what she had just witnessed. Should she call the police? But then again, she thought, why should she? She now knew that monster had in fact murdered her mother, stolen her father's name, and gained her trust by pretending to be him. Of course, she still didn't know why he had gone to all that trouble and may never be sure why he had left Singapore to come to find her. But he was gone, and she felt that her mother had at least had some justice, as had all those countless, nameless people he had murdered or abused.

Chapter 26

Karma

Adrienne returned to her hotel, asking the receptionist to make up her bill, as she would be leaving in the morning. She noticed the woman looking at her face, where he had struck her, but she said nothing, and Adrienne wasn't about to enlighten her as to what had happened. She ordered a sandwich and coffee from room service as she realised that she hadn't eaten since the morning at the Café Rouge.

Once in her room she stripped and showered, trying to remove every last trace of 'that monster' as she now thought of Armand Bouchard. Then she packed her belongings, ready to leave early in the morning. All she wanted to do now was to go home.

She slept only fitfully, her dreams full of swirling water, his face, her mother's face, and the violence she had witnessed in the park. She eventually checked her watch and it was seven o'clock.

She had decided that, before catching her train, she must visit the Garden of Remembrance in the Pere Lachaise Cemetery, where Janey's ashes had been scattered. It seemed the least she could do. She wouldn't be able to give her a proper funeral, but she could leave some flowers there in her memory.

She quickly washed and dressed, and made her way to the Marche aux Fleurs to buy some flowers to take with her. She picked up a Paris guide from the newsagent's and then returned to the hotel to pack her things. Studying the guide she could see that the nearest stop on the metro was Gambetta, and that the Jardin du Souvenir, which even she could work out was the Garden of Remembrance was close by the nearest entrance to the metro station.

Going down to reception to check out, as she approached the man behind the desk, he said

'Ahh Madame, I have some things for you. They were left at reception for you a few minutes ago.'

He handed her a large brown envelope addressed to her. She thanked him for it, wondering who on earth could have left it for her. Could it have been the police? Maybe they had found more information. He also gave her a small white envelope which she realised was probably M Blanc's bill. She would send him a cheque when she got home, she decided. Determined to open the large envelope later in private, she placed it in her holdall.

After settling her bill and thanking him for the service she had received while staying there, she left and made her way to the metro station at Les Halles. She could see that with one change she could soon reach Gambetta. As she emerged from the station, she followed the signs to the cemetery and soon found herself standing in front of the Jardin du Souvenir monument.

She stood for some minutes, taking the time to think about Janey and the twists of fate that had brought her to her final resting place in this foreign land. She shouldn't be here, she thought sadly, she should be at home, with her mother and Marge. Unsure where, exactly, her mother's ashes had been scattered, she decided the best thing to do, was to leave the flowers in front of the monument, and she laid them carefully down. She softly murmured 'Goodbye Mum'. Then on an impulse picked up a handful of soil and wrapped it in tissue. She thought that she would place it on the family grave back home, supposing that it might bring her some closure. Placing it carefully in her holdall she took out her hanky, wiped the tears from her eyes, then turned and walked back to the entrance of the cemetery.

Ten minutes later she was back on the metro, making her way to the Gard Du Nord. Checking the timetable when she arrived, she saw she had an hour to wait until the next train to Calais, and decided to grab some breakfast, and then, to open the mysterious envelope.

The contents of the envelope were not what she had expected. There was an official looking form, made out as though she herself had completed the details. It seemed to be a claim form to cash in an endowment in her name. She realised the envelope must have been in the document case the men had picked up last night, and she was grateful to Lauren for passing it on to her.

She looked to see if there was anything else in the envelope, and there at the bottom was a postcard which explained about how a safety deposit box, held at a certain bank in Paris could be opened using numbers engraved on a bracelet which had been sent to Janey Grainger. The contents of the safety deposit box were to be for Adrienne Grainger when she reached the age of twenty-one!

As she read the postcard, the final pieces of the jigsaw were beginning to fall into place. That's why he had lured her mother to Paris, to bring him the bracelet! She didn't know how he did it, but it must have worked. The endowment was what he'd been after all along. Of course, in 1962 when he opened the box he must have found the information about the endowment. He would have been livid that he couldn't claim the cash because the endowment was in her name! The report of Aunt Marge's death must have prompted him to try again, now that she was over twenty-one, and that's why he had turned up at the graveside. She was thrilled to think that this postcard in her hands had been written by Francois, her father, and that she had meant enough to him, to leave her a legacy.

She looked in more detail at the form. So how, did she wonder, had he intended to get her to hand over the money to him? As she turned over the form, there was the answer. The bank details at the end of the form for payment of the monies, were not hers, but his. She supposed he would have told her that once the money was paid into his bank he would transfer it to her. So for nineteen years he had been scheming to get his hands on her money, and had even been willing to kill her mother for it, but now he had gone, and the money would be hers.

Adrienne boarded the train to Calais and as it sped through the French countryside, she reflected on the sequence of events that had led to this moment.

If Francois and his wife hadn't had an accident, Bouchard wouldn't have stolen his identity and eventually lured her mother to Paris to bring the bracelet Francois had sent her years earlier. If her mother had chosen not to take the bracelet to him, she would not have died. If Marge hadn't had an accident Bouchard would not then have turned up at her funeral. If she hadn't come across Janey's postcard at that precise time, while Bouchard was still around, maybe she would never have come to Paris herself. If she hadn't been in Paris with him, Lauren wouldn't have approached her to help them capture him. If they hadn't, he may well have escaped justice forever and she would never have known how her mother really died. Now he was dead. She felt no remorse for the part she had played in his downfall. All the evil things he had done had come back on him in the end. Justice had been done. It was karma, she thought.

Later, as she strolled around on the deck of the

Cross Channel ferry heading back to Dover, with the white cliffs sparkling in the distance, and the seagulls wheeling overhead, she felt a peace and calm she had never felt before.

She knew what had happened to her mother, and where she had died. She knew who her father had been and that he had cared about her, making provision for her future before he died. She must still face a life without Marge, but she now felt strong enough to carry on alone.

Somehow, she knew that all would be well.

The End

About the Author

Marilyn Freeman enjoyed a rather varied career pathway, starting out as an Industrial Chemist and progressing into entrepreneurship, manufacturing toiletry products among other things. Since retiring from industry, she has spent several years editing and publishing books for her husband and writing and creating life-story and poetry books for various private clients. Karma is her debut novel.

Marilyn enjoys writing about people and the interaction of differing personalities. She loves to take a long look at the lives of her characters and is fascinated by the way apparently simple decisions can cause effects that resonate across generations, sometimes with devastating results.

If you have enjoyed reading Karma, why not check out Marilyn's second novel, **Secrets and Lives.** It explores the unintended consequences stemming from a young woman's decision to give up her baby for adoption in the 1970's. Although she took the decision in order to give her child the chance of a good life, as is so often the case, good intentions do not always produce the desired result. When her child, now a grown man, re-enters her life he brings tragedy in his wake. **Secrets and Lives** will be available to purchase from all major retailers from 5th **June 2021.**

Contact Marilyn Freeman:
email: inbox@marilynfreeman.org
facebook: www.facebook.com/marilynswriting
Website: https://bit.ly/37uNt1d
Author profile : https://bit.ly/3bpfsR8

DISCUSSION GUIDE

I hope you enjoyed reading KARMA as much as I enjoyed writing it. Here are some suggestions for you to use as a discussion guide within your reading group:

How did Karma make you feel?
How do you feel about how the story was toldy?
What did you think about the main characters?
Did the characters seem believable to you?
If you were making a movie of this book, who would you cast?
Which parts of KARMA stood out for you?
Would you read another book by this author? Why or why not?
If you got the chance to ask the author of this book one question, what would it be?
What do you think of the book's title? Does it relate to the book? What other title might you choose?
What did you think about the ending?
What themes did you detect in KARMA?
What is your impression of the author?

Thank you for reading KARMA, and for taking the trouble to discuss it within your group.

Marilyn Freeman

Lightning Source UK Ltd.
Milton Keynes UK
UKHW012117250321
380989UK00002B/86